The Inter-Twinning

The Inter-Twinning

By

Heather E. Hutsell

The Inter-Twinning
Copyright 2009
1st edition

Although the characters and events here within are fictitious, the authoress does not guarantee that the reader won't notice some similarities within themselves to one of the characters. In the event that this is the case, the authoress strongly hopes that you will find that she has captured your finest qualities.

ISBN 978-0-578-01843-0

~*This book is dedicated to all siblings*~
By blood or by heart
We unite.

Chapter One
Ianto and Seamus

January 19th

When Ianto and Seamus were born, Ianto was a
complete breech birth. His twin Seamus was an Occiput
posterior birth, and a complete surprise to their parents, as
they had been certain and assured by the midwife that Ianto
was alone in the womb. As it turned out, Seamus not only
followed his brother, but he was pulled out along with Ianto,
who'd had a steadfast hold of Seamus by his bitty hands. They
were born two months prematurely, healthy, and otherwise in
the usual way. Though whether Ianto was trying to bring
Seamus out into the world or Seamus was trying to keep Ianto
out of it, no one but the two of them would ever know.

Chapter Two
Aubrey and Audrey

March 19th

When Aubrey and Audrey were born, they were in transverse lie presentation until the very last possible moments. They were in a great disagreement on who would be born first and so a second and last argument ensued at the brink of labor. The girls twisted and turned and turned and wriggled around until they were sufficiently entangled in their umbilical cords. This posed a great and unknown danger for them both, for their mother was so unaware that her contractions were more than a little stomachache that she did not bother to get to a hospital. She was quite surprised when her perfectly identical twins practically slipped right out of her as she stood in line at the local bakery, baguette in hand. Even at seeing their blue-pale bodies back to back and at such a difference, they refused to even cry, their mother did not budge to retrieve them. They were quickly scooped up and wrapped in flour-dusted cheesecloth by the pastry chef and handed over to their mother, who was reluctant to give up her enormous bread stick to take them in arms.

Chapter Three
Beau and Bonnie

October 13th

When Beaureguard and Bonnaventure were born, it was by an emergency caesarean section. Their mother had been in a horrific and planned car accident, leaving her without breath and quickly following without life. The twins were also presumed dead but when someone thought to check, it was discovered that they were in fact safe and unharmed. When their mother was cut open, the twins were found locked in such a very tight embrace, that they had to be carefully removed from the womb in the most delicate of unions. Complete separation was fated to them on their birth day, and it was as though they had already known this before ever having taken their first breaths.

Chapter Four
Georgina and Gabriel

December 8th

W hen Georgina and Gabriel were born, not only did they nearly deafen their attending witnesses with their screams of protests for everything that was happening around them, but they terrified and perplexed everyone present as well. They had fought with one another from the earliest moments possible after conception and while still in the womb—over space, over nourishment, over oxygen, and their combative sparring resulted in Gabriel pushing Georgina out first with several hearty kicks to the bottoms of her feet. She made her appearance in a normal cephalic presentation. Of course, his insistence on her being out of his way did not result in Gabriel finally having the womb all for himself, but rather it brought about his own uncalculated footling breech birth. The birthing staff on hand, as well as their mother and father, were horrified to see that they were both head to toe covered in black and blue bruises. It was after some very extensive testing and screaming and waiting that the cause for these wretched purple marks was ruled inconclusive.

Chapter Five
Ianto

It was somewhere near half past three in the morning when Ianto was shaken awake in his bed. He had been having a dream of a shiny wooden dowel as it turned and turned on a lathe and he watched as it became a gloriously shaped spindle. At first he had thought that something was wrong with the machine for it shook so terribly, but it became apparent that it was in fact his and Seamus's nanny who was rousing him. He rose at her command, dressing sleepily in the clothing she tossed to him, feeling sick to his stomach for having been awakened before he'd gotten his full rest, and watched with gritty eyes as she did the same to his brother.

There was scant time between their waking and their departure and so little explanation was given for it. Ianto gave his twin an uncomfortable glance and he knew that Seamus also knew—whatever was going on had to do with their absent parents. They would still know little to nothing, even as the car they traveled in pulled up to the nearly deserted northern docks and they were taken aboard a medium sized whaling ship. Few words were said to them as they were deposited into a closet of a cabin. Then, with only a kiss to each of their cheeks from their once doting governess, they were shut in for the rest of the night.

When the door opened only a short time later, Ianto and Seamus were again awakened, and this time by their new guardian. It was quickly explained to them that their parents were now dead due to an unexplainable and tragic accident involving a door harp and a slab of drywall. And now, as the ship was set for the Arctic, they were to remain in the captain's care until they came of age, or until further notice. With this, there would be plenty of promised hard work, but their new parent was seemingly kind and fair. Seamus and Ianto were thankful enough through their dreamy and foggy state that they weren't going to be taken from one another. Having observed their condition, the captain left them to get what little rest they could, for he was to be back again in a few hours' time so their day could begin.

15

It was shortly before these few hours had passed that Ianto awoke on his own, cold and shivering in the gray light, and the reality of their circumstances hit him. He climbed into his brother's bunk and shook him roughly, the fear of their being alone and suddenly stolen away rising to its full density.

"Seamus!" he whispered loudly.

"What? What is it, Iant?"

"Wake up, Seamus—"

"Why? It's not time to get up yet."

"*Get up*—" Ianto persisted. He waited a moment then, knowing that Seamus would come around. It took only seconds and Seamus's blue eyes opened fast and wide. He sat up, his stare locking onto Ianto's.

"Were we--? Did we--? Are we--?" Seamus did not know what to ask first.

"Yes! What are we going to do?" Ianto lamented. He did not wait for Seamus to catch up, but ran to the porthole and looked out: there was nothing but cold, gray water for as far as the eye could see. As he stood there, hoping that land would show—as though he could will it to, Seamus got up from the bunk and was already putting his shoes on. Ianto sighed.

"Don't bother with that," he said gloomily. "We're not going anywhere any time soon."

Seamus found a crate to stand on, for he was not quite as tall as his brother and he needed the wee bit of added height, and he dragged it to the porthole so he too was looking out into the bleakness.

"What will we do now?" he asked his brother.

"It appears that we are in for the long haul of it."

When the captain sent one of the sailors for the boys, they were already in their coats and waiting patiently on the bottom bunk. The man who opened the door and beckoned for them was a giant of a human, red-haired and mute. He seemed monstrous, but far from frightening and Seamus and Ianto went with him without question. They were taken above deck and set out with instructions on swabbing the gopher wood. This was odd to them in a way—it seeming like such a thing to happen on a pirate ship in a fantasy story, but for the fact that it was windy and cold out there and it was growing ever colder by the knot. They did as they were told, pausing only to blow hot breath on their cold and reddening fingers and to dunk their mops into the water buckets, breaking and rebreaking the thin ice that formed on the surface. After a few hours, they were let into the galley to warm themselves and to eat. The captain joined them at the table then.

"Do you know what kind of ship this is?" he asked them, his thick white mustache covering his entire upper lip. Both boys shook their heads. "This is a whaling ship. That is why it is so large. But we do not hunt the whales for murder, you see. We hunt them to study them. And do you know what we have found?" More shaking of their heads ensued. "We are learning that whales—of all types, mind you—are in fact far more intelligent than even we are. Now is that believable?" Seamus and Ianto looked at each other, confusion written all over their little faces. The captain answered for them:

"It is true. You two seem rather intelligent yourselves—perhaps you are part whale?"

Another exchanged glance between them. The captain humored them and took a photographed whale in a frame from the wall next to him and held it on the tabletop for them to look at more closely.

"This here is a Beluga whale." He took a pocket watch from his vest beneath his coat and opened it to reveal a mother of pearl face with delicate roman numerals on one side, and the face of a toddler on the other. "This is my nephew. Does he not look like the whale?" They had to admit that the baby did have a similar face, especially since they both appeared to be smiling and both the child and the whale had matching large blue eyes. Still, it seemed a little silly to the brothers, but if the captain said that whales were intelligent, then he must be right.

"Will we see whales like that?" Ianto asked, hoping that this man was not a speak-when-spoken-to sort of adult.

"You may. But what we are looking for on this voyage is something a little different. Now I'm not going to tell you what they are exactly or what they look like. I am going to let you two watch for them and you can tell me when we've found them."

This seemed quite eccentric and wonderful to the brothers and certainly they were not in any sort of disagreement about it. They had both done quite a bit of study on animals and sea life in their schooling and they were confident that they would be excellent observers and dependable partners in the venture.

Ianto was trying to hold his spyglass steady to his eye against the violent chattering of his teeth, so he could continue keeping watch for whales—or whatever great thing they were supposed to be on the lookout for. So far, they had yet to see anything, though they had been at sea for three weeks now and both he and Seamus were getting more and more discouraged despite their captain's reassuring that they need not be, for they had to take the time to travel far north first. It was not likely that they would see much right away.

But it was at long last their mute friend who made the discovery of the first sighting. He bounded across the deck and grasped hold of Ianto and Seamus's coat collars, half-pulling and half-dragging them to the starboard and bringing them up to the railing. At first the boys did not see anything but snow and ice floes and deathly cold water. But as the moments passed and the ship slowed down, for he had signaled for the captain to turn off the motors, they began to see movement that was more solid than the water and ice. It was quite suddenly that a very long, ivory colored lance shot up through the slate water, and it was followed in succession by a dozen more just like it, and just as many blackish, white and blue-splotched torpedoes came up attached to the lances. It was baffling and mesmerizing to watch, but Ianto and Seamus could not look away. They could not even find the words within their mouths to ask what they were looking at. They did not need to.

"And there they are—" said the captain, who had come up behind them to see the whales, for he had marked them from where he'd been steering the ship. "And look at them—a good few too."

"What are they?" Ianto was finally able to ask, still unable to look away.

"Those are narwhals," the captain explained. "Watch them now—"

The animals seemed to stand in the water, circling and swirling around with one another in a sort of a ritual dance. They were tightly huddled, their long tusks waving a bit and tapping together and the entire scene was so gentle and beautiful, tears went streaking, undetected down Ianto and Seamus's faces.

"What are they doing?" Ianto whispered. The captain bent down close between them and spoke softly.

"They are talking to one another. Just like we do—but more peacefully."

They remained there for as long as the narwhals did, watching, appreciating and falling in love with what they were seeing. The captain was respectful of their awe and said very little, for he too loved the sight of their sacred meeting.

Though the entire experience lasted a good part of an hour, it seemed like mere minutes, and then the whales dipped back under the water and their pod swam away, their long, twirled teeth sticking out just enough that Ianto and Seamus, the captain and their first mate were able to watch them long into the distance.

The captain put his hands on the boys' shoulders then and sighed, the sound of rejuvenation and a warm smile in his voice.

"What say we go below deck and warm up a bit? And how about lunch?"

They were in agreement over this and the moment they were within the galley, they were wrapping their cold little fingers around warm, tea-filled Victor mugs. The boys were given hot chowder and broken off chunks of sourdough bread to eat, which they did, both of them famished. The captain sat and ate with them as well, studying them for a moment before speaking.

"I know that I've not asked it of you yet, but tell me about yourselves," he instructed of them. Ianto and Seamus looked at one another, not sure where to begin—they were so young and did not know what kind of information mattered to this near stranger.

"What do you want to know, sir?" Ianto asked, timidly.

"Anything. Everything. If you are to be my wards, then we ought to know one another, don't you think?" They nodded. "Start with your ages. How old are you?"

"We're eight," Seamus offered.

"The both of you?"

"Yes, sir."

"Well now that is interesting. You are twins?" More nods. "Well, you look nothing at all alike. I never would have guessed that. I would not have even guessed that you were brothers, had I not been told of it. Were you in school?"

19

"Yes, sir," Ianto said this time. "The fifth year at primer school."

"Smart boys then?"

They both smiled, proud that their marks had all been excellent.

"Well, there now," the captain remarked. "You have the very same grin as one another. You do look like brothers when you are smiling." To this observation, it was hard to stop their beaming. "What did you excel in?"

"Math," Ianto said.

"And drawing," Seamus added.

"Drawing?" The captain's interest peaked with his raising brows. "What kind of drawing?"

"Buildings and castles and those sorts of drawings," Ianto said.

"Are you both good?" They nodded more. To this, the captain rang a bell and his first mate appeared. He instructed the loyal man to bring him two pencils and a large sheet of drafting paper from his cartography room. When the man came and left again, the captain gave his instruction to the boys:

"I want you to draw something for me—anything you like, any kind of building. But I want you to start on one side—" To Ianto. To Seamus: "And you on the other and meet in the middle."

This of course sounded like great fun to Ianto and his brother and they both took up a pencil at once. The captain took a large, stiff card and stuck it in between the boys so they could not see one another's work. At his word, they began and the captain sat there with them, watching as they concentrated, created and designed and drew.

It was two long uninterrupted hours later that Ianto and Seamus finished their drawing, both of them setting down their pencils at the same time. Their guardian was fascinated, awestruck, impressed. He ran his hand over his mustache, and shook his head slowly, uncertain as to what to say. Instead of saying anything, he removed the card so they could see what the other had done:

On the paper was one building joined by two halves. It was completely different from one side to the other, but they matched perfectly. Ianto had drawn a large church-like structure with beautiful large doors and Mandela stained glass windows. He had labeled that the building was made of mahogany and cherry wood, the windows were of black and red and crystal and white glass. The doors were of ebony. Seamus had drawn a similar foundation to the building, though his gray stone sides drew up higher at the top, creating a steeple of an attic, the pinnacle of it a gentle arc rather than a skewering spire. Hanging off of the side of the building was a rounded and extending room—a turret of sorts. He had labeled that its walls were made entirely of beveled Herkimer, even the roof of it, which sloped on all sides and resembled a thick double-ended quartz. The brothers were very pleased with their complementary drawings.

"What is that room for?" the captain asked of the turret.

"I don't know sir," Seamus said.

"Well, whatever it is for—whatever the entire thing is for, it will be something very grand, and great things will happen within its walls."

And so it was to be: every night after the brothers had done their chores, sightings had been seen, their supper had been devoured and they had finished their less interesting subjects of learning, they were permissed to spend the evening drawing up their amazing ideas. The captain was faithful in looking them over, asking questions of them and making sure that they included each and every detail regarding their materials, their size and their whereabouts, were they ever to spring up from the ground somewhere. They did not end their drawings when they left the table each night however, for once they had retired to their cabin, they would share a broken tip from a scavenged narwhal tooth and a coveted bottle of indigo, scratching slow and careful lines into pieces of discarded wax paper. These sketches they kept hidden between the chest of drawers and the wall for protection, for once their other drawings were done, the captain took them away and put them into a hiding place of his own. Ianto and Seamus could not imagine why. Still, it did not stop the boys from further developing their skills at it, nor did it at all hinder talk of their mutual dreams of one day making these buildings something real to look at. It was a pact that they fabricated between them: that they would travel both educated worlds and the world itself to study even more, and eventually live out their shared arrangement of becoming the creators of the greatest structures ever built.

They had but only one shared haunting.

"Do you ever think of her?" Ianto asked Seamus in the middle of the night, months later, not expecting him to be awake to answer, but he was.

"Sometimes." Silence passed between them. "Do you?"

"I try not to," Ianto admitted.

"Me too."

"I can hardly remember what she looked like now. And when I think of Da, I just see the captain."

"Me too."

"Do you think she thinks of us? Wherever she is now?"

"Probably not."

And this reoccurred, many nights along their years, their constant hope and fear alike that the questions of their mother would someday be answered.

Much time passed and as much as Ianto and Seamus had grown to love the sea, the voyages and their captain and guardian, they both began to feel quite restless, not ever getting to set foot on solid ground for more than a few days at a time. They began to wonder if theirs on that ship was the only life that they were ever going to know so long as they drew in breath. It was not much longer after they began to have those uncertainties that their answer came by way of a very unfortunate incident.

Ianto was the first up between himself and his brother and this was not unusual outside of this particular day. He stirred Seamus by pulling his blanket off of his brother's frame, smiling as a groan came from the sleepy being in the bunk. He did not wait for Seamus to rise before he left the cabin and went above deck to begin his work. He was barely a foot onto it before the first mate took a hold of him by his collar for the millionth time, and hurried him to the captain's quarters. Ianto knew by the grim look on the man's face that something was terribly wrong. He went into his guardian's cabin, finding that it was dark but for a dim lantern and it was cold enough to see one's breath, which was quite out of the ordinary for the captain. Ianto found the man lying abed, his gray eyes half open, and he went to him at once.

"Ianto—" he called with the weakest voice Ianto had ever heard come from the man. "Where's your brother?"

"I'm here—" Seamus said as he came through the door in a rush, still buttoning his shirt and trying to walk with his boots only mostly on. He made it to the bedside, both he and Ianto suddenly fearful of the news they were about to hear.

"Boys—" They drew closer to their foster father, taking hold of his hands, which were turning blue at his fingers' tips. Already, they could scarcely detect any life left in them. "In two days' time, you will be returned to land," he began. "I have made arrangements for you for a place to stay, and you will not want for anything." Ianto and Seamus looked at one another briefly, deciphering what was meant of this. "I have made some connections for you, where your schematics are concerned, and when you get settled, I want you to see to it that you make these works of art realized—" The first mate brought a protective tube out from a wall safe, and handed them to Ianto and Seamus—each and every one of their drawings had been carefully rolled and stored away in it for safe keeping.

"Are you coming to land with us?" Ianto dared to ask, though he knew well the answer to this.

"My boys, you do not need me where you are going and my days are done. You are young men now and you have your own course to follow. I am just grateful to have been some part of it at all. You make me proud and you will continue to make me proud. It is rare that a person gets to see the things that we have seen out here in the sea—beautiful and surreal as they are. You are going to do something of the same, but in your own way, and make it possible for others to experience things great and beautiful. And I'll have no decision from either of you to the contrary: *you will make these happen.*"

It was then that Ianto and Seamus made their good-byes to their captain and guardian for before the day was passed, he fell asleep forever. They were to leave the cabin then as the first mate was to prepare him for his funeral, but they refused to go. Instead, they helped to wrap him from head to foot in cloth bindings and at sunset, he had a captain's burial at sea.

The twins spent the rest of the evening in the galley, looking over their drawings and keeping their conversation quiet. They had been assured that their futures were secure and all they had to do was step into them. Though saddened by

23

their sudden loss, they could not help but be optimistic and hopeful for what lay ahead, nor could they fight their eagerness to get started. It was enough that their captain had believed in their visions as much—if not more, than they did. It did not matter much that when they set foot onto land for the first time in a long while and to begin their new journey that they were barely sixteen years old.

Chapter Six
Aubrey

The lack of maternal love only worsened, for it was bad enough that their own mother could never tell them apart. She had never really made the effort, this was true, but they were not for her to try to accept. She was never going to even try.

Aubrey stood in the doorway of the hallway to the living room just as her sister Audrey stood in the doorway of the kitchen, looking in as well. Their mother sat on the couch with her hair in a terrible disarray of dirty, rattiness and badly needing a touch-up to straighten out her highlights. She was dressed in the same denim skirt and misbuttoned stained white blouse that she'd been stuck in for days, and she was stubbing out a hastily smoked cigarette, breathing quickly and lighting another before the other was even completely out.

"It's just—strange, you know?" she was saying to the girls between her inhales and exhales. "It's strange, and I can't take it anymore."

Aubrey and her twin looked at one another, their lavender-blue eyes locking but they said nothing, and they simply stood still, Aubrey twisting the curled end of one border albino platinum pony tail while Audrey twirled the end of a braid.

"You've been doing it since you were both babies— ever since I found you sitting in your crib at nearly only three months old—just *staring* at one another and having a complete silent conversation between yourselves. But you never stopped—you still do it. I know you do. You do it in school, you do it in church—" She looked from one of them to the other, tapping the ash onto the carpet, not caring that it singed the olive shag.

Gone. Thought Audrey.

Totally. Aubrey thought back.

"—And you are doing it now, aren't you?" their mother accused, seeing their thoughts cross between the twins as though the words were just particles in the air. She huffed and shook her head before taking a long drag. "Well, since

you won't stop, and I have told you, and your teachers have
told you *a million* times to cut it out—"

Uh-oh— Aubrey thought.

Big uh-oh— Agreed her sister.

"—I am not going to beg anymore. I refuse—*do you
hear me?* I absolutely *refuse* to ask again. So now, it looks like
you've really left me no other choice." And here she paused.
Because she didn't want to say it? Because she didn't know
how to phrase her words? Merely it was to finish out her
cancer-inducing smoke in a long sigh of an inhale. "Pack up
your junk. You're leaving. Today." Had there been any less
emotion in her voice, the twins would have thought their
mother to be a robot.

Is she serious?

Looks it, doesn't she?

Serious as a heart attack.

Aubrey giggled at the pun.

"STOP IT!" A heavy root beer colored glass ashtray
went flying through the air, sending a gray stream of snow
behind it before it hit the wall and landed with two severed
thuds on the floor.

*Looks like a face—*Aubrey thought of the black mark
left on the wall.

*Maybe a panda's face—*Audrey countered. *Or a biplane—*

"*Get-out-now!*" screamed their mother. But it was not
all of the screaming or the marathon smoking or even the
throwing of the ashtray that startled them and brought them to
attention—it was that their mother was suddenly pulling her
hair out by the fistful and clawing at her own face with ragged
fingernails. She seemed to be trying to hold in an unleashed
rage, but could not rein it in completely. She could scarcely
keep her teeth-clenched screams from turning into glass
shattering shrieks.

"Momma, stop it!" Aubrey cried, running to her side
to try to stop her. Her mother resisted her attempt at
comforting and shoved her daughter hard enough to make her
fall head over heels over the coffee table. Audrey was at her
sister's side in a blink, helping her up, helping her to regain
her bearings.

This is really, really bad!

What do we do?

We have to go! We have to go now!

"*Out-Out-Out! Get-out! Get-out—!*" screamed their mother, as she rose from the couch.

The girls ran to their shared room and pulled their matching tapestry suitcases from beneath the bed, and as they heard their mother's raised screeching from behind the closed door, they packed as quickly as they could. There wasn't much that they could take with them in their small bags, nor was there much time to be selective, for as they were shutting the little latches over poorly chosen clothing and little useless, sentimental trinkets, and taking the window and lattice wall to the ground outside, they could hear objects of unknown identity joining the ashtray in slamming against window and wall.

Once safely on the ground, they paused to catch their breath and to think: just where exactly were they going to go?

I don't know sissy, but anywhere but here.

Should we go to gramma's?

Even gramma is scared of us—Aubrey pointed out, knowing that this was indeed true.

Yes, I suppose. And she is insane. God, I can't believe mommy snapped! So where then?

I don't know. Let's just get going.

And they did begin to walk very quickly away from the only home they had ever known. They did not look back, not wanting to have the memory of what was happening to or within their house. And though they did not see it, they both knew as the distance spread between them and their only other known relative, that just as the many cigarettes had in those last few moments, their own mother was surely as well going up in flames. But there was nothing they could do now to stop it. And there was no one that would be able to offer any sort of help. They knew they would not stop talking to one another as they did since before birth. No matter who asked and no matter what happened. It was just their way and it was the only sanity they could maintain between them in a world that did not understand.

The journey that Aubrey and Audrey made that day was very long. They were exhausted from their walking, they did not know to where they were going, and they had very little money between them. As they walked they discussed their options and as usual, they said nothing out loud for anyone around them to hear. They did not worry that anyone would bother them, for they could tell just from the looks that people offered them, that they would not be approached for any reason. They knew that they were odd and they knew that everyone was afraid of them. Their pale white-blond hair and their mysterious and unusual eyes—the terribly uncanny *exactness* to one another, were all enough to set anyone aback. For once, they were quite thankful for this.

It was well into their trek that they made their way to a train yard and in good time, for it was becoming quite dark. There were no streetlights where they were now and neither of them had foreseen to bring a flashlight. This was now no concern to them and as they just wanted to get off of their feet and rest for a while, they were very pleased to see an empty boxcar on the rails. There were many more cars there along with the one they climbed into, but they only needed one for their shelter and at that moment, any one of them would do.

Do you think we will be okay in here?—asked Audrey, as she lay her head on her suitcase, facing her sister.

We won't be found in here—Aubrey promised. *It is so dark. We'll just get up early in the morning, as soon as it is light and keep going.*

They had not to bother waking to continue their trek, for long before the sun rose and as they were both still fast asleep, the train began to move and it carried them right along with it.

It turned out that the train that Aubrey and Audrey stowed away on belonged to a traveling circus. They found this together as they felt the motion of the car, and as they sat up to take a look at their now sun-lit surroundings, they quickly realized that they were no longer alone. Sitting quietly at the other end of the car were a few of the contributing performers: a bald man with a very long and thin black mustache, which he was taking great care to curl the ends of with wax from a tin. He was wrapped in a leopard print sarong and he wore gladiator sandals on his otherwise bare feet. His muscles were gratuitous and his head shone as though he had waxed it as well. Next to him was a very tiny woman with shiny beetle-black hair that she had pulled back into a bun on top of her head, with half a dozen spit curls framing her petite face. She wore a red and black ruffled Spanish flamenco dancer's gown and she was compulsively stringing and tying red rosebuds tightly together to make a chain of them. Sitting on the floor of the car was a tan-skinned man wearing a bright pink satin turban and a yellow pair of Turkish pants. He held a small squirrel monkey on one arm and she clung to him while looking the girls over with care. Lastly, there was a great black, orange and white striped beast lying next to them all, panting and purring loudly even over the noise of the metal on the rails.

What should we do, Aub?—Audrey began. The monkey noticed them fully awake and bounced across the floor to them, pausing to stand on her hind legs and to tilt her head inquisitively.

Do you think it's safe in here? Not that we can do anything about it now--

"There is no harm to you here," the man in the turban assured them. He clapped as the twins exchanged a glance in wonderment, for certainly he had read their exact thoughts, and the monkey obeyed his command, returning to his side. The man gave the monkey two bananas of which she was to deliver to the new arrivals. Obediently, the creature did just that, pausing at their sides, not wanting to give up such a nice breakfast, and she even attempted to put one of them inside of her blue velvet vest, though it was poorly and inadequately hidden there.

"Manners." At the single word, the monkey handed over the fruit and waited patiently for a reward, which came from both Aubrey and Audrey, once they had broken off a sizable piece of banana for her. She did not hesitate in running back to her master, her treasure in hand going straight to her mouth. Finding that they were both quite hungry, Aubrey and Audrey did the same. Once finished, they sat up against the wall of the car, looking at the other passengers and the two beasts, their words to one another continuing.

Where do you suppose we are headed? Audrey wondered to her sister.

I don't know. But I think they may be part of a circus. Why else would they have a tiger outside of a cage?

As if it had heard them, the tiger gave a soft roar and nodded its head in acknowledgement. The girls looked at one another in astonishment—they were certain that the animal *had* heard them!

"You do not seem to have a plan of some place to go," the turbaned man observed. The tiny woman went closer to the sisters and offered them a bottled beverage, which they graciously took. A few sips of it proved that it was refreshing and tasted sweet like violets.

"No," Aubrey said honestly. "We have nowhere to go."

"Do you have any talents or tricks?" the man asked them. "Aside from speaking to one another without your voices—"

The girls looked at each other again, their eyes wide.

"How did you know that we could do that?" Audrey asked, looking at him again. He shrugged at her question as though it were only natural for him to know it of them.

"It is plain to see as it is in your eyes," he explained. "Can you do it without looking at your sibling?"

It occurred to them both at that moment that when they spoke together in their special way they usually did look at one another while doing it. Could they without doing so? They did not know. Eager to try the experiment, Aubrey and Audrey turned to have their backs together.

This is kind of silly–Aubrey said to her.

I wonder where the little monkey came from— Audrey thought to her sister.

I can't believe how fast this train goes and that strong man and the little woman don't fall over from it!

Do you think there is any more food?

"Turn to your twin," the man instructed. Once they had done so, he continued. "You have much work to do on that," he professed. "You do not follow one to the other with your minds without using your eyes."

The girls were surprised to hear such a remark, but as this was indeed true, then they were keen to learn how to develop the skill. They were also quite curious to know how this stranger knew that they were not connecting successfully with one another in that position.

"There will be plenty of time for that later," he said, as though he were latching on to their separate thoughts as well.

It made them only a little uneasy to have him so interested in their way of communicating. Aubrey felt that changing the subject was best for the moment.

"Your cat is very tame." And certainly she and her sister alike were glad for that.

"He is very well behaved," the man agreed. "And do you know how this is done?" He sent the monkey back to them with two bunches of grapes. The girls accepted them and afforded a few each to the deliverer.

"How?" Audrey asked.

"He has been trained, without the use of whips or cages," he said. The girls looked at one another in astonishment. "They learn more effectively this way and it gains their trainer greater respect, and so they are more likely to act with obedience."

"And how is that?" Audrey inquired. "How do you actually train them then?"

"Just as you and your sister there speak to one another, so do we who train the animals." He paused to turn to the tiger and pet it on the head. This was not to be believed.

"Speak to him now," Aubrey requested.

"Very well," said the man. "I will ask for his paw—"

The two of them had a moment of silent conversation and the tiger tilted his head to one side before lifting his right paw to be taken. The man did so with both of his hands, and gave it the slightest shake before nodding to the great cat with salutation and setting the paw down. The tiger only began to pant and look around, quite content and relaxed.

"There you see. Quite intelligent, as you will find— they all are."

"And what would happen, if one of the animals acted up?" Aubrey asked, peeling one of her grapes before eating it.

"They will not."

"And what if one of the workers strikes an animal?" Audrey asked, knowing that neither of them ever had any worry of that.

"Then they will be cast out, never to return to the circus." His answer seemed enough for them and they finished up their grapes.

"You are without exception, exactly alike in appearance and voice," he said then, sending the monkey back a third time with some bread wrapped in a cloth. "How is it you are told apart?"

The sisters looked at one another, realizing then that no one had really bothered to try to tell them apart. They were so precisely alike in looks that even though they were not conjoined, practically everyone who encountered them just took them as one entity. They shrugged.

"Audrey hates to wear shoes," Aubrey offered, though her sister sported them for the journey. "And I hate to be barefoot."

"As you wish it," the man said.

"Where are we going now?" Audrey asked. "Is this a circus that you travel with?"

"We used to travel the world as a circus," he explained. "And now we are going to our last place of performing."

The twins were disappointed to hear that the circus was ending. Of course, they had misunderstood and this was not at all what the man had meant by his words.

"We have been built a new place in which we will operate, and we will no longer travel to the people: they will travel to us."

"What kind of a place is it?" Aubrey asked.

"We have never before seen it. We know only that it awaits us, and in two days' time, we will see it for ourselves." He studied them for a silent instant. "You will be joining us there?"

The girls were intrigued by the idea of it. They hoped no one would be coming for them, but how would they be found wherever it was that they were going? From all they had ever seen in movies or heard about of circuses, if someone wanted to run away and hide, it was certainly one of the best places to go.

"It is there for you to think about," he finished. "As it is new and never used before, know that there is plenty of space, we are told. Your own private quarters will be waiting for you, do you wish to stay on."

The thought of becoming a part of the circus was intriguing to the girls. And a rescue come in perfect timing. Certainly they wanted to stay on!

Once the promised two days had passed, the train slowed and finally stopped. Aubrey and Audrey took the temporary steps out of the boxcar and huddled close beneath a dark blue cape. They had been caught in a rainstorm but it was only a few feet to the awaiting caravans. They wondered for a moment where the tiger would ride, for the tracks and train had stopped a few miles from their destination. They hoped that he would not have to walk the distance in the rain. But their unasked question was answered when they saw the strong man open the back door of a sedan and the great cat jumped into the back seat. The man got into the passenger's side in the front and the driver took them away.

The caravan that the girls sat in looked to belong to gypsies, because just as everything else was that they had seen so far in relation to their new life—it was also very colorful. It began to move shortly after they had climbed inside of it with a few new travelers, and they took the ride in silence, not even communicating with one another, for they were lost in their own thoughts. They were on their feet nearly the very moment they stopped, running to the windows to look out as the others did, for the captivated expressions of the others drew Aubrey and Audrey there with curious interest.

In the near distance stood an enormous structure that shone blond-silver even in the overcast daylight. It was their new big top: frilly, elaborate and looking like one gigantic Chinese paper-cut doily that had been pulled up by its pinnacle so all of its beautiful cut-outs could unfold and be seen. It was like a colossal three-dimensional snowflake and they could scarcely believe that they were about to go into it. They began to walk with the group, slowly, wondering if it was just a dream they were moving toward. As they approached and became closer, they were able to observe the incredible detail: gargoyles and knaves, queens and cherubs all in its workings. There were scalloped edges, club and spade shaped dagging; windows of colored glass in masterpiece form and impersonating works of art. Windmill blades spun from various points around the edges and the girls thought it looked to take off and fly away if it so desired to.

Aubrey and Audrey followed their new workmates in through the doors, and they all stepped into the beautiful vestibule. It was decorated with miles of navy blue velvet and swarovski crystal, which caught any little bit of light that came through and bounced it back. The twins felt as though they had stepped right into nighttime. They continued on into the arena and it opened up into a glorious room, the size of it swallowing them up in its enormity. Before they could spend too much time there, their tiny woman companion took hold of their skirt hems and tugged them in her direction. They went with her and they were introduced into a private dressing room. It was decorated in pale pink lights and plush coral velvet vanity chairs, and two matching loveseats at opposite ends of the room. A cherry wood armoire stood in one corner

33

and there were plenty of mirrors, as though they were inside of an elaborate jewelry box. They continued on through another door within the dressing room and they found themselves in a bedchamber fit for an underwater fairytale: there were two beds in the room, both of them round with shimmering jellyfish canopies. The two matching dressers were shaped like seahorses that stood one and a half times their height, and the drawers pulled out from the seahorses' bellies. The windows covered the entire length of the rounded-out wall and they were filled with aqua, cobalt and teal glass blocks. Strands of large ivory freshwater pearls hung in the doorways that led into a small kitchen area and their own private bath. The bathtub was of clear glass and shaped like the fattest goldfish that they had ever seen—two steps were required to step up into it.

They were thankful to have such a comfortable and fantastic room. It was such a dreamlike adventure that they now found themselves in, they hoped that they would not awaken and have to relive the catastrophe that they had only a few days ago left behind. Even as those presiding over the paperwork came around and took what information the girls were willing to offer up, the surrealism of it did not fade.

Training began early the next day without a moment for reprieve. Audrey and Aubrey were introduced to their new boss and guardian, who was a young, kind woman and a sibling of seven, and who was graciously happy enough to take them under wing. It was only vaguely explained to them that everything within the big top—including the two of them and the woman herself—now belonged to those who had created their new home and place of work. Who that was exactly, was a great mystery, but no one thus far had had any objections toward it—everyone being so well accommodated, and so the girls did not think that they would balk either. They were finding as the day went on and as they adjusted to their change, that they were thankful to have a safe place to sleep and that they could count on there always being something to eat when they were hungry. Their sweet guardian confirmed every bequest, assuring them against their fears that they would be well protected and cared for, and never would they have to be afraid of any unfortunate happenings, so long as they were there.

After breakfast and their pleasant visit, they were given a quick tour of the entire place, which took little less than an hour to cover. They were introduced along the way to anyone who happened to be about: the acrobats, the animal tamers and charmers, the daredevils, the oddities in appearance and those who were odd like the two of them; the funny merrymakers and the mysterious. At last, they were taken to a room that was floor-to-ceiling black. The furniture was of ebony velvet that absorbed the light, and the illumination in the room was a cool blue that came from large hanging paper stars. They were instructed to each take a seat, facing one another and Aubrey was instructed to look at the images on the cards before her, one at a time. She was to then imagine it in her mind and Audrey was to guess it. When they went through eighty or more cards, getting every single one exactly correct and in detail, they were told to turn back to back and to do the same with another set of cards with images. For this, they failed every last one. When they were released for lunch, they stormed back to their water world room, frustrated and upset that they had been blocked from one another's minds when it was usually effortless to communicate wordlessly.

Why couldn't we do it? Audrey wondered, while they were eating eggplant and mozzarella sandwiches.

Maybe we weren't concentrating hard enough—

But eighty cards, Aub? Eighty? That is ridiculous! Not a single one right! Not a solitary one! That's simple kid's stuff and we couldn't do it!

"But you will—"

They looked to their doorway, startled by the intruder who now stood there unannounced. It was the turbaned man.

"You will practice and practice every day and all day until you master it. And with time, you will."

It seemed a little anomalous that this man was encouraging them so to do this with their talent, but they could not shun the idea of it, for they too wanted to have the skill perfected. It could do them no harm.

And so they did practice and practice, until eventually, they were able to sit facing away from one another and have a conversation together. It was quite another lesson they had to learn once they started having to try it from different rooms.

In the meantime, the twins were taught to hone their levels of agility and balance. They practiced the tightrope with a young man, who had mastered it despite having only one leg, and they played on the trampoline, and at a very low level, they learned to use the trapeze. Their study with the other acrobats was much more fun than it ever was work, and within months the new circus was ready to open up to brand new patrons.

It took only a few nights for the success of the circus to reach the farthest corners of the world—by the end of the first week, every seat was filled—and there were thousands of them—and patrons were even willing to stand in the aisles to watch the show. Not only was it the first non-traveling circus, it was also the first one to have a bear that could knit while riding a bicycle and bats that could tap dance while wearing tiny tap shoes. Even the twins were fascinated by these two acts and they made certain never to miss them. When it came time for them to perform, Aubrey and Audrey stunned and startled the attendees with their ability to know what the other was thinking. They disproved each and every accusation of a hoax by involving the audience members and as none of them who were chosen had ever been there before, every display taken on a bluff was shown to be as real as the skeptics themselves. They became quickly well known and they began to appear on the billing as "The Golden Twins", for their same-said hair and their ability to fascinate their viewers. They wanted never to leave that place. They hoped that it would never be taken from them, or they from their wonderful home, so perfect their lives had become.

Chapter Seven
Beau

Beau sat on his heels behind the monks on a very cold and hard stone floor, listening to them chanting out their prayers. He had been there with them for the entire five years of his life so far and though he knew a dictionary's worth of Latin, when they chanted it just sounded like mumbling. Still, it was soothing and when he closed his eyes, he could no longer feel the aching in his knees. Instead he felt his spirit rise to leave the great hall they were in, passing over the labyrinth of mosaic tiles behind them on the floor, and it would take a walk outside. He could always do this, and he could always see things exactly as they really were just outside of the monastery walls without ever budging a muscle. It really was his favorite time of day—this chanting, his most favorite activity that they involved him in—aside from when he was allowed to help attend to the bees.

The apiary was in the front of the grounds, just beside the dirt road that lead to who-knew-where. There were many times while Beau stood there with the little winged creatures, covered head to toe with canvas and netting, and holding dripping honeycomb that he wondered just what he would find did he go down that road. His imagination would go rampant and he dreamed that did he ever take it, he would see many interesting and amazing sights, which not even the books he read could wield. He knew that he would see these things some day and not just in his mind.

And then there were his own private dreams that he kept locked up tightly to himself. Dreams that were constantly haunted by the face of a girl that he swore he knew but whose name always escaped his mind's grasp at just the moment that he thought he would remember it. He also thought about her while tending to the apiary. He could hear her laugh when the bees were buzzing softly and he thought he felt her breath near him when the bees would flutter their wings close to his face. He could detect her scent in the fragrant sweetness of the honey and the taste of it—warm and gentle and alive: it was enough for him to almost have her there with him. Beau knew he would see her someday, and he knew that he would know her immediately, whoever she was. For many years, Beau felt that he would see her there at the monastery—though perhaps it was only because of his dreams. And though no women were allowed there, he still envisioned her beneath the full diamond garret, for that was his favorite room there. If he could ever bring her there—*when*—he corrected himself, when he brought her there—he would give her that room to stay in. Of course, this was not his room to give. It was where special praying was done. When very lost souls made their way there to the monks, they were given special blessings in that room— for they had been told that the designers of the monastery had wished it to be used for something unique. Whenever Beau was able, he crept into this room and gave special prayers for *her*, for in his heart he knew she needed them more than most because she was lost. At the very least: she was lost to him.

Yes, when the day came, and he knew it would, he would be certain that this room was for her.

When Beau finished his work each day, which he always found to be more therapeutic and meditation-inducing than actual labor, he would take a heap of paper or canvas and pencils or paint with him to the nearby shore. There, he would finish out his afternoon with the invention and creation of a new visual world of some other dimension. Sometimes he would paint abstract landscapes or scenes of the lost emptiness of his insides—which sometimes were one in the same. Always, his thoughts would gravitate to the mysterious girl with no name and a face he could not clearly see. His skills and talent improved naturally, untutored, and though he even tried to paint her a few times, the best he could ever do was to outline a figure for her in jet and embrace it in violet. Some days he just accepted this. Other days he could not, and on these blacker days he would tear up his papers and burn his canvases, and throw stones at the waves as though it was their fault and they were erasing her clarity like they erased the discrepancies in the sand.

It was on the day that this behavior and frustration peaked that one of the caring brothers approached Beau about it. He could not hold it inside any longer: the dreams, the visions, the incredible and forelornful yearning, and he gave in and told all. He had feared that he might be shunned for these thoughts, or cast out—discarded as someone unholy or unworthy of any longer being there, for he could not stop any of this from happening anymore than he could have stopped the world from revolving. But once Beau had explained his expressed emotions and with it calmed enough to catch his breath, the supportive monk gave his direction:

Beau was to leave the monastery for one year to find this mystery girl and save her in whatever way he felt would be best for her. If in that year he could not, he was to give up the search forever and think no more on it. It would be the Lord's will that she would be found or not and he was greatly advised to trust in this.

Beau was not just fifteen years of age but there was no question in any part of him that this counsel was astutely given. He was quickly packed up, given a head start in funds and with the parental advice to take care and write often, he set out on his impossible pursuit.

Days went by, stretching out into months and it was a hunt akin to searching for a needle in a haystack—ever more challenging still: a *golden* needle in a haystack, because it was so precious that he should succeed. Beau hadn't the slightest idea of how he was going to find her, for the world was greater than he was and greater than he could ever have imagined. And he had nothing to go on but hope and the tugging in his heart and soul, and the knowing—always the knowing that he would recognize her the moment he saw her.

He worked odd jobs for food and places to stay, traveling from one side of a country to the other, from one side of an ocean to the other, never stopping, never giving in. It only occasionally struck him that perhaps his being released into the world might not have been the wisest or safest of decisions made by his guardian, but still it did not at all occur to be the wrong one, as no harm ever found its way to him. In fact it seemed that each day became easier for Beau, and though nothing ever came of his searching, his feet never tired and his mind never grew weary. In truth, the more the days passed, the more refreshed he felt, and trusting in this at long last brought Beau a very great reward.

It was late May and comfortably warm and though he had not broken his fast that morning, Beau pushed on with renewed energy and perseverance. By the afternoon he was looking out off of a cliff's edge over an ocean's shore that was new to him. It crashed and beat the rocks below, but the sun was shining and the gulls swooped and played overhead. The breeze was blowing warmly and the air was refreshing and salty, putting new life into Beau's lungs. And then he saw her.

A petite frame stood on a huge boulder, cloaked in a plain brown tunic too big for her that whipped violently about her legs in the wind. Her long chestnut hair was wild and loose about her though her little white hands worked hard to clear it from her downcast face. Beau felt his breath catch and his heart leapt in his chest because it was she—he *knew* it was she. It was as he was making his way down to the beach to her, that the ghost of his dreams saw him as well. She hastened her way to him, feeling the pull within her own heart. There was absolute recognition in her eyes for him—the blue-green of her irises as though she'd drawn the sea into them, locking with the brown of his and holding. As he felt himself swelling large enough inside to hold the entire Universe, he also became panicked that something should stop them from meeting, and he might not get to her—

But nothing stopped them and they met, entwining, becoming as they had been last they were together. Beau scooped his Bonnie up in his arms and held her so tightly her breath was as swept from her lungs as her feet were from the ground. Her heart pounded now with his and her soul was restored, and her own thoughts connected with his spoken words.

"On my life I will never let you be taken from me again!" he whispered to her, feeling her arms tightening in return. He put her down and drew away enough to take her face in his hands and shower kisses all over it, taking away the tears and seeing her smiles replacing her sorrow: she had been waiting for him to come to her.

When Beau returned to the monastery with his sister, he was met with a disturbing site: the monks had been busily packing and moving what little belongings they had there, and already the thick forest of trees that surrounded the building was being cut down. No one quite knew how it had happened, but the bordering property had unknowingly exchanged hands, and though the monastery property was safely untouched, houses were going to be built in the area by the dozen. This was no longer an appropriate place for prayer.

Beau was exhausted from his journey, Bonnie nearly dead on her feet and the only thing they desired was to clean up and get some sleep—certainly this was not how they had wanted to be welcomed in!

Beau's companion was then noticed by the head brother as they were greeted at the door, her head covered with the hood of a long black coat and her face hidden in the shadows of it. The brother was suddenly amazed at realizing that his young ward was not alone and he had in fact succeeded in his quest. Had the man ever any doubt in the power of the heart, he certainly did not now! He moved aside and they entered the foyer, the brother touching Bonnie on her arm gently.

"This—is she?" asked the bewildered man.

"Without a doubt," Beau stated in answer. Then to his sister: "Bonnie—"

She lowered her hood and the man with them could see at once that there was a striking resemblance. He was sorry that the brotherhood had already made arrangements to leave in the next few hours leading them into dawn, for he would have enjoyed spending a longer time with this reunited family. And no matter that it would have by the rules been forbidden, he would have made a way for her to be there with Beau. As it all had turned out, they'd been blessed to be kept in one another's care. And for this the holy man was not so saddened that he was put in the position to leave his own home. He knew better than to ask them along: this pair of siblings knowing better than he how to survive now.

Before they were left behind, Beau was helped in bringing a bed into the praying turret for Bonnie. He had in the past feared that he would not be able to keep her in there, nor keep her hidden as one of the others in the monastery at all, until he could make other living arrangements for the two of them, but he now had no concerns of that. It seemed that their worries were diminishing into fewer and fewer.

Bonnie sat on the floor in the candlelight after washing up, watching as Beau made up the bed for her, and it was not long before the last of the monks had left and only the siblings remained. She was nearly dozing off, despite how excited she was to have been brought there. And now, having her twin back in her life—she hoped she would recuperate quickly so they could get better acquainted with one another. Their journey back to her new home—their home now—had been light in the way of conversation, the high of their reunion having stolen all words away from their mouths, leaving their communication mostly in smiles. There were so many years to catch up on and still she could think of nothing to tell him, but that her prayers had been answered by his discovery of her.

Beau finished with her bed and gently roused Bonnie to help her to it. She crawled into the softness of the berth, Beau having made certain that she would have only the very most comfortable accommodations, and he covered her up to her chin with the warm blankets. She reached out to him and he sat beside her.

"What will we do now?" she asked him. "Will we have to leave here too?"

"We aren't going anywhere," he promised. "This is where we will stay for as long as we wish to. I am not sure how, but I will find a way to keep it that way."

"Was this your room?" she asked, already forgetting that there had been no bed in it when she had arrived. There had been nothing in it at all but candles reminiscent of her past in their tiered rows. But now that she was lying down, it was hard to keep her sleepy thoughts from swirling.

"No, love."

"What was this room then?" Bonnie inquired drowsily.

Beau explained the room's purpose and how he had stolen into it so many times before bringing her there, so he could put precious thoughts out into the Universe for her. She only half heard what he was saying, content just the same to be listening to the sound of his voice. He could feel her drifting off to sleep under the gentle stroking of his hand through her hair as he unbound it from her long braids. He smiled at her, also feeling complete for the first time in as long as he could remember.

"I will tell you more in the morning," he vowed. "There is so much more to tell you," he added.

"Stay in here tonight," she whispered. Her eyes opened halfway at him. "So I will not fear that you've gone away in the morning. I don't think I could bear to awaken and find you and this to all be just a delusion."

"I wouldn't dream of leaving," Beau said, his heart swelling. "And I will stay in here tonight."

He promised to return in moments, Bonnie making him swear many times over before he even reached the door that he would hurry, for she did not want to drift off completely until he was back. Beau held to his word, slipping into the narrow bed with her soon afterward. He kept a candle burning so he could engrave every detail of the image of her face in his mind—he did not ever want to forget it, not even once his eyes closed for slumber. For the years and lifetimes that had passed since they had last been together, it only felt natural for them to rest in such a way, for as they had been in the womb, so in life would they be. They stayed close, their hands clasped together between them in a silent, mutual pledge to one another. It was very soon after that when sleep came for them both and for the first time in a many, many nights, Bonnie did not dream.

When Beau awoke in the morning and for every morning after that night, he was greeted, whether at his side or from a doorway by Bonnie's smile. Together, they were able to find ways to stay in the monastery—Beau selling much of his artwork to eager buyers and Bonnie took up her pen, writing out her dreams, writing tales of frightening monsters, of romances between lovers and mysteries to be cracked. It was rare that Beau did not find her beneath piles of paper and her left hand—and sometimes up to her elbow of the same arm—covered with smudges of ink. It was a while before she would allow anyone to see her stories, for she was horrified at the mere thought of it. But Beau naturally was the first to see any of it, and even this was by sheer accident.

He had been sitting outside with her on a rather pleasant but breezy day, and he had tried to persuade Bonnie to take her loose papers inside for fear that she might lose hold of them and they would be lost forever. He knew from her having lost a single page once before by unknown means that this would indeed lead to the irrevocable death of whatever she was working on, and so he put great faith into his warnings. It was not in vain, for on this particular day, an unexpected gust did hit, and as she was just flipping a sheet of paper to frantically scribble on its blank side, the bluster took it and another right from her hand. In an instant, Beau was on his feet and chasing after it, Bonnie momentarily stunned but quickly following after him, fearful of the papers' loss. He pleaded to the elements that they not get too far away from him and as if to hear his request, the wind plastered the papers against a wall of tall golden grass, freezing them there but for a protesting and vibrating ripple of one corner. He swiped them up in his hand, sorry that he wrinkled them some in the process. He then held them in the air with a wave, showing her that he had proven her hero in rescuing the white, fibrous rogues. On his way back to Bonnie, he had lowered the sheets and the simple sight of her penmanship caught his eye. He had not intended to *read* what was written, only to study her letters and how her silly upside down way of holding her pen had created the script among the smudges there. But the words were too captivating: *I have already sacrificed—*

He could not help himself. He had to read more:
Again, I have sacrificed.
And so you have.

And before he knew it, he had finished reading the one side before turning it over and reading the other.

When he reached Bonnie, who now eagerly awaited him, her pen pressed to her lips as she stood, her other papers in her other fist and tucked up at her side, he lowered the sheets and gave her a tilted and guilty smile. He was hooked.

"I am sorry, love," he said sincerely, offering up the rescued papers. And after a pause while waiting for a reprimand that did not come, he raised an impish brow and said, "Do you have any more?"

He could not have expected a scolding from her— perhaps anyone else, but not her. She smiled, her nervousness at her work being seen now shattered. But this was not just anyone—this was her precious and trusted Beau and she handed him the rest of the story in her hand as though she were handing him her life. He immediately sat in the grass and set to reading it, not stopping even as the daylight grew dim and his eyes had to strain in the dusklight, until he had finished.

With Beau's encouraging and gentle pushing, and after begging her to allow him to read even more, Bonnie released her work to him and then to those who could help her take it to the next level. For this, the twins found themselves to be comfortably and independently wealthy within their first year together. Beau said it was because they had been able to give one another strength in their creativity. Bonnie believed it was because their reunion made them twice as able to do anything they set their minds to doing. There was no doubt that it was one in the same and they were both right.

Time passed and as much as she loved their home, which had become more of a lived in residence for the two of them than a monastery, Bonnie began to miss the opera house near where she used to live. Beau asked her to tell him more of it, for she had never before mentioned it to him in her time there.

It had been an immense building that was constructed on the same property as the convent she was raised in, some time in her infancy, and this was where she had lived since she had been divided from Beau. Its purpose, so she had been told, was for the money it would raised to help the convent continue on. Bonnie wondered of course, if the nuns had not been up to something else but had never dared to question it. It had been an instant success—just the mere sight of it alone being enough to draw people from all over the world to visit it and take in its image. Many who showed there spoke of it as a great privilege, and despite its greatness, the true meaning of this to Bonnie was not entirely clear. It was rare and usually only during inclimate weather that there were not at least a dozen artists sitting outside of it, creating in their own way its portrait. The performances that went on inside were just as stunning: *en pointe* ballets, operas in honor of the building's interior decorum, classic performances, new and *avante guard* acts, symphonies—it was a great luxury to have the opportunity to indulge in the theater's offerings. Bonnie was never privy to enjoy these moments and could only steal away into it when the opera house was closed. She told Beau that she had spent many hours daydreaming of a different life while being in it, as though it had some sort of magic that could make her dreams real. Beau was fascinated by his sister's descriptions of the place, though Bonnie had her own favorite parts about it. She hoped that some day she would have the chance to see it again, though it made her disheartened to think that she would have to go all the way back to where Beau had found her in order to see it. She did not think she could bear to do so, for the fear of somehow being left behind there. Beau assured her that this was a silly thought—he'd as soon leave behind his head and heart and soul than leave her to the ungrateful and undeserving nuns. He would be sure that she would see it again and enjoy it whenever her heart desired it, somehow, without any risk of that.

It was becoming less and less frequent, but still the nights came when Bonnie would awaken, with or without tears in her sleep-closed eyes, and being alone in her beautiful room, she would grow needlessly frightened by the shadows in the corners. She would seek Beau out on those nights, respectfully knocking on his door if it was closed and freely entering if it was not. She would never express surprise when Beau would have a lover with him, almost as though her fears over countered any shock or embarrassment she might have had at the discovery. Her invasions were never taken by her brother as such and there was never a time that Beau would refuse her need of his comforting. He would simply sit up after bidding her to come in, rouse his bedmate and explain to the sometimes-bewildered companion that they needed to leave immediately. If they dared to give any sort of protest, he would stop them with a few simple and indisputable words:

"*Bonnie comes first.*"

And as this rejected lover was on his way out, Beau would open his arms to Bonnie and bring her into the warmth of his bed. He would kiss her forehead and stroke her hair while holding her close, and ask her what it was that she had dreamed. Sometimes she would say—sometimes not. Then he would tell her that everything was all right and she was safe, and always she believed that to be true.

And then there were times, though infrequent, that Beau would seek her out, though rarely was it because something had worried or upset him. Simply he would be looking in on her late into the night to be sure that she was well and that she soundly slept—and that she had not just disappeared, or been stolen away by an admirer she'd had no interest in. Truly, that was his greatest fear in life—that Bonnie would be taken from him, for any reason but for the sake of meaningful love. Her own lovers, though few and far in between, always showed dotingly enough at first—her great heart always misleading her from caution, and when their affections proved false or shallow, she would retreat into lengths of solitude. Even from Beau. It was murderous, he thought of it. But he would not interfere with her relationships—only be there to rejoice with her when it called for it. Or help to put her back together when her world shattered.

Sometimes it was a beast—their being siblings, for though never had a woman since Bonnie lain at his side, nor would one ever again, he would have staked his life on it that no one could love her as he did and always would. He was grateful for her wanting him to have his own room within his tower. Not for fear that he would ever compromise her inappropriately, but for the fear that he would want her all for himself, forever forbidding any other man from her bed and her embrace. If only he could protect her from those who would deceive and hurt her, but her choices had to be hers alone.

He could do nothing to change this but make his random visits to check in on her. Always, she would lie so still and scarcely look to be breathing there, hair splayed across her pillows, some kind of white satin gown or other that she wore making her look like a sleeping ghost-angel in the four-poster bed that was far too big for her alone. He would be overcome by the deepest desire to be a part of that peaceful perfection and without making a sound, he would steal in under the covers, never awakening her, and then he would draw her into his arms. If she did wake, she never let him know by more than sighing and relaxing into the posture of him, her leg trapping one of his under it, and he would not dare move until morning. When she would open her eyes and discover him there in the daylight, she would lie on her side and look at him, never wondering why he was there. And when he was with her, it only seemed right that he should be.

Chapter Eight
Georgina

While in their incu-beds in the hospital's NIC-U, and at two days of life on the planet, Georgina and Gabriel were inclined to make horrible faces at one another through the Plexiglas that separated them. When they arrived to their new home, aged two weeks, and were put into their shared crib for the first time, their parents were awakened in the night with such shrieking from their tiny newborns, at first they feared that their pet cat had gotten her foot caught in the dog door again. They quickly discovered that it was in fact baby Gabriel who was crying at the top of his tiny lungs as his sister lay sweetly and silently awake, her feet over his face. They could not figure how Georgina had turned herself around into this position, for when they'd been placed into the crib, they'd been side by side. It did not end after one, or two or even a dozen incidences: by two months, they had to be separated into two different cribs, for unless they managed to kick at each other until they ended up at the opposite-most ends of it, they threatened to keep the household awake every second of the night with their fussing.

At their second year, Georgina and Gabriel's parents held a very elaborate party, believing them to be old enough to enjoy such a gathering. Every child in the whole of the neighborhood was invited and gifts were piled high on a table in the back yard. Georgina was dressed in a short white puff-sleeved dress of eyelet, a yellow giraffe on the bibbed yolk of it. Gabriel matched her in a short-legged romper, an elephant on the front of his. They were a perfect picture and to everyone in attendance, they were spit-shine flawless with not a hair out of place.

The party commenced and games were played, food served up. But when the time came for the cake to be cut and plated, neither twin could be found anywhere. A great panic erupted and just as a search party was being formed and readying to set out after the guests of honor, they heard one loud and startling shriek followed by relentless giggling. Everyone rushed into the kitchen to find Georgina and Gabriel both on the tabletop—Georgina laying across the blue, pink and white frosted double sheet cake, Gabriel sitting on his sister's back, while holding her face down in the confectionate chaos. When Gabriel had been removed from her and Georgina had been removed from the cake, her face was a colorful and sugary mess, the frosting so thickly coating it, her wide eyes could barely blink through it. Gabriel pointed at her and roared with laughter again.

"*Yeti!*" he cried at her, laughing so hard he fell onto the floor and nearly had a seizure. Georgina saw no humor in it at all and she gave herself a moment to catch her breath while the crowd dissipated. The very moment everyone had turned their backs, she dumped the entire contents of the ice cream punch down on top of him. The incredibly loud splash caught their mother's attention and she rushed to the scene from the kitchen tap, the tiny washcloth meant for Georgina's face completely insufficient for the fiasco that she now faced—a mountain of snow and ice blue and a pool of grasshopper green.

The fighting and screaming only grew worse as they grew older. It was constant and relentless, neither of them ever seeming to run out of the energy it took to put forth such a battle. A surefire tip off to rousing their war was when anyone remarked how very alike they were and that they resembled small, constantly contrary, screeching birds when interacting with one another. They would insist, Georgina and Gabriel— and death was preferable to it—that they were not a thing alike, though this was quite despite the fact that their hair had turned midnight black and that they had the exact same jade green eyes.

"You know, you are the biggest pest *ever!*" Georgina said, referring to her minutes-younger brother. To this accusation, the twelve year old shrugged and whipped his mangled, well-read comic book at her. It only made half of its way to her, flipping around like a withered eighteen-winged pixilated insect. This gained a disgusted growl from her and she chucked a handful of clean underpants from her laundry at him. Gabriel dodged it well enough, shielding himself with the ruffled pillow from her bed on which he lay.

"Now *that* is ghastly!" he said, sending the pillow in a volley.

"What are you doing in here anyway?" she asked, picking up her strewn garments.

"Annoying you."

"Well that is for sure!"

"*Well that is for sure!*" he mimicked, turning on her rose comforter, muddy galoshes shirring across the spread, before he picked up her locked diary and began trying to pry it open. She immediately heard the incriminating sounds and she filled with anger.

"*You Little Fuck!*"

Georgina pounced on her brother and with one hand, grasped his Pan-curly hair and punched hard between his shoulder blades with the other. Despite the assault, Gabriel held onto the precious little book with a death grip, finding that the more his sister beat on him, the more her ire made him smile.

"You are *sadistic*! You are a *jerk*! *You* are pointless!" she was screaming.

Gabriel could only laugh, and when he got free from her, he took the book and ran with it into the bathroom. She followed only as far as the doorway and saw him standing with it in his hand, dangling it over the toilet. Gritting her teeth, Georgina stormed, fuming into his own room and found his most prized possession: an autographed photo of himself standing next to Errol Flynn. It had been a chance meeting and ever since, Mister Flynn had been Gabriel's hero—she knew there was nothing in Gabe's possession worth more to him. Georgina made sure that Gabriel saw her holding it high above her head and he watched her as she backed down the hallway with it toward the kitchen. She stopped when she stood next to the stove and she turned the gas burning flame to a high flickering blue. They could see one another perfectly from where they stood, both of them frozen and awaiting the other to make a move to justify their own premeditated revenge. It was clear that neither of them was going to back down, even when their front door opened and a mutual friend came right into the center of it all. He immediately saw them and what they were up to and he gave a great rolling of the eyes.

To their shenanigans, he had only one thing to say:

"You two are the *worst* twins in the entire Universe!"

He stayed for only a moment more and when neither Gabriel nor Georgina moved a muscle but for their evil grins

50

to grow ever more, their friend gave an exasperated huff and left with a crashing closed of the door.

"You give?" Gabriel asked.

"*Not ever*," she sassed. "You?"

"Don't count on it, sister."

"*Whatever!*" Georgina roared, before dropping the photograph onto the flame. It curled up fast like a dry crackling leaf and Gabriel felt his own rage peak. He slammed Georgina's journal into the water, the weight of it making a messy splash as it hit. For good measure, he pulled the chain flusher over and over again. His sister narrowed her eyes at him and roughly flipped off the stovetop knob, before she came racing down the hallway at him, a dishtowel in hand.

Gabriel snickered.

"Lot of good that will do you!" he said, referring to the cloth. Georgina did not flinch, but stuck the dishtowel's end in the toilet water before snapping it in Gabriel's direction. He attempted to move, but she was faster and the towel hit his cheek, leaving a long red stinging lightening bolt of a mark. He caught a corner of the cloth before she could strike again, thrusting the plunger at her and when the towel wrapped around it instead, he yanked it from her grasp. Unarmed, Georgina turned and ran, slamming her bedroom door in his face and ramming a chair back up under the knob.

"You're too slow, jerkface!" she yelled at him through the door.

"Just wait, hag!" he said back to her. "You have to go to sleep some time!"

"So do you!" she shouted in return. "I'd keep your door locked if I were you!"

Georgina and Gabriel were always just short of burning the house down, breaking bones or otherwise causing a great disaster of one another and their home. While they would always right their residence in plenty of time before their parents ever found out otherwise. And though they had a peculiar unspoken pact that they would never assault each other in the face, their bodies would persistently be covered with bruising. It was quite a wonder, considering how Gabriel and Georgina treated and felt about one another, that Georgina's interests lay in a caring subject matter: when they were not quarreling and beating the tar out of each other—and being one argument away from hating one another—she

51

talked continuously of one day taking in discarded or hurt animals and having a great place for them to live. Gabriel thought her to be ridiculous. Their parents thought her to be adorable. But she swore that if she could trade half of the world's human population for talking animals—starting with her brother—she would do so in a heartbeat. She was sure to study as much as possible in all matters of biology, zoology and she made special studies of land animals. By the time Georgina was an adolescent, she was an immovable vegetarian, forsaking any and all meat from her diet and all leather from her wardrobe. Of this, Gabriel thought her absurd. Their parents thought her charming, knowing that in a matter of a year or two she would grow out of her phase: this was not ever to happen.

Georgina prepared as well as she could for the day that she would leave home and have her sanctuary. Her animals would be protected and preserved, loved and living. She would not let this dream go, no matter what anyone—least of all Gabriel—said or believed. She had all of her ambitions—she needed now only to find the perfect place in which to carry it all out.

Chapter Nine
Seamus

It was what he had wanted to do his whole life, he thought. At least it was what he had hoped to do ever since he was able to put images down on paper. And now, Seamus was realizing: he and his brother were finally getting to do it for real. It seemed like a dream to him then—even as they were discussing blueprint plans with the contractors who were going to make their creation of mahogany and gold gilt, plush maroon velvet and lights not unlike the sun come to life. He wanted terribly to stay and see it built, to help direct the uprising of the structure as some day soon a director of a great stage performance would do the same with his or her cast of actors on the soon-to-be-built stage. But they were only delivering the ideas and perhaps one day they would see the results of his and Ianto's visions. There were so many of them to bring to life, there wasn't going to be any time to wait around—and that was the only part of it all that made him sad.

Seamus unrolled the blueprints again, for the hundredth time since they'd been placed in his hands and he studied the white lines on the blue. He saw that Ianto had added another story of balconies, making a total of sixteen above the mezzanine level, and the uppermost floor had a hidden passageway leading to it by way of secret doors. *Rooms for lovers*, he presumed and knowing his brother's romantic heart, this was very likely exactly what they were. Seamus walked his fingers across the drawn stage, admiring that they'd chosen to add a side-winged rostrum so the actors and actresses and other performers could half-encircle their audience instead of just facing them straight on as most stages required. Some day they would just have to see this for real, perhaps even partake in a performance there. He could not imagine exiting his life without fulfilling that part of his dream. Until then, for him they would seem incomplete.

It did not make sense to Seamus, why *she* always came up when he was lost in thought—this envisionment a woman who no longer had a face for him—just an image, sometimes a voice and rarely a scent of *Jontue* cologne accompanying—especially when his thoughts had to do with his and Ianto's dealings and not anything that *she* had ever contributed to them. Was that fair, to think that way of her? It wasn't her fault she invaded his thoughts. And it wasn't to her credit either. He could not imagine her having influenced the creative process for their designs—they were so unlike what she would have been fond of. At least, what they had known of her. Maybe there had been a hidden side to her. Maybe she was speaking to them of such ideas from beyond. Seamus still doubted it. But as these thoughts always carried on, he could not stop the associated reminiscence:

Seamus and Ianto had been sitting with their captain on the ship, finishing up their breakfast.

"Boys," he had said. "I want to talk to you about something."

They had sat in silence while their guardian puffed on his pipe, the cherry vanilla tobacco smoke so delicious they could almost taste it.

"I heard you talking in the night about your mother, and I want you to know that she was truly a fine woman." It had struck them as odd when this had been said, for never had anyone spoken of her to them before or after that moment. "She would have been thinking of you. She thought enough of you before she died to be sure I would have you, should something happen to her—"

Seamus had thought about that most of all, going over it and over it again and again in his head. They had never overstepped the unspoken bounds of asking the captain how he had known her and he had never offered to say. It was the only regret Seamus had on the matter, if it could be called that. And so the only conclusion Seamus and Ianto could draw of the captain's sense toward their mother, was that when either of them looked to the stars and she crossed their minds, they would be overcome by an intangible sense of nostalgia and they would study each star as though they would hold answers of where she might be just then, and who she really was. They could see that it was the same for him—that he would be caught up with the same sort of lost and distant look in his eyes, and it left them all three with a silent wondering of *what if?* Never again after that one time did he say another word about her. And never after that did they ask.

It was as though the stars had told them everything and at the same time, told them nothing: if only the stars had told them of what was to come years later.

Seamus was about to venture off onto another reflection when Ianto burst into the room, a beaming smile on his face and a roll of papers in his hand.

"What's that?" Seamus asked smiling as well, for Ianto's excitement was infectious.

"While I was talking numbers with the suits in there, I talked them into fronting the *Tower* Project, the *Monastery*—*with* the garret you designed, *and* the *Sanctuary*. The only one left to market is the *Big Top* Project and they're looking at that one right now!"

"Wow, that's incredible—"

"Yes! They want to get them up as soon as possible. As soon as we decide where we want them built. They'll do whatever they need to do to get us the locations we want as well! *Anywhere*! And you know what that means, don't you?" And before Seamus could answer, Ianto finished: "It means we can really focus on finishing the *other* project. You know—the fun one!"

"They're all fun," Seamus corrected, amazed that so many of their ideas were drawing such fast investors.

"Yes, I know, you're right." Ianto clapped his brother on the back. And after a silent moment, Seamus smiled too and gave him a hug of congratulations.

"This is really great!" he agreed. "It really is."

As surreal as it was for the brothers to be watching by as their dreams became a reality, Seamus was always disappointed—as he was positive Ianto was too, that they were just never getting back around to see the finished products of their imaginations. Always, they were able to inspect the materials, to be there for the breaking of ground, even to receive extensive and detailed photographs by post, as it was required by their contracts. But it was just too difficult to drop things and travel backwards—new projects always seeming under way and the constant preparations for them taking them away and away and away. And they knew the photographs could not do justice to the real thing, no matter that they were professionally and assuredly *perfectly* done.

Instead of letting this depress him, Seamus continued to help his brother with the designing of what was to be their favorite of them all—a grander, secret project. He thought that perhaps what they were devising for it was extraordinary—maybe too much so, sometimes. Ianto insisted that it would not be impossible to make it real—that it would come about just as the others had, and were they not seemingly beyond conventional grasp? Had all of their investors thus far not been astonished but eager to have a share in them? It was just that it would out-do all of their other projects, and even Ianto had admitted this. Yes, this one was to be very special indeed. So much so, that Ianto did not want anyone to take it on as a private contract for construction: he wanted to be there and with Seamus's help, they would watch every bit of it take shape—they would *insist* on it, and anything upcoming after it would have to wait until this other project was completed and they saw it done with their own eyes. They would eat, breathe and sleep this one, and if this meant that they would raise their own hammers to create it—if it meant that it would take years longer to complete it, then so be it—they would do exactly that to be sure that it was entirely theirs.

Until then, the travel turned out to be great fun for them both. They would go to all ends of the earth to scope out possible places for their masterpieces, making sure that every detail of every location was absolutely perfect.

Seamus and Ianto found that they loved to fly by plane or by zeppelin; they loved traveling by train. They grew melancholy and nostalgic when they had to take boats, but still, they would do it: because they had made their promises and would not fail on them.

It was rare that they were able to go home for too long at a time, but occasionally they would. And it was almost always a guarantee that something unusual would happen there—most often these instances were good.

But this particular time, Seamus brought in the mail and amongst the usual paper fodder were two heavy and elegant envelopes: one in navy blue for Seamus and the other in deep red for Ianto. He gave his brother his mail and proceeded in opening his own, finding that the envelopes both contained only a single matching card with urgent and important instructions on them:

November 30th   11:30 Post Meridiem
Bring your enclosed charm and do not lose it—
No matter what.
Be prompt.
Do not, under any circumstances, disregard this invitation.

An address was listed for where they were to show and though neither of them had ever been there before, they knew that its general location was not much more than a short plane ride away.

"Not too much time between now and then," Seamus muttered to himself. "Only two weeks, is it?"

"That is kind of a remote area, isn't it?" Ianto was asking his brother, while holding an enclosed lock up by the cord it was on to better look at it. But Seamus had other thoughts going on, mostly in regard to the strung key in his hand. He felt a mixture of dread and anticipation at what it could mean.

"You *do* know what these are for, don't you?" Seamus asked and Ianto nodded despite not wanting to. "I wonder who finished the design?"

"I don't know," Ianto muttered. "I don't want to know. I don't think I want to see this." Even as Seamus was handing the invitation to him to look over, he knew that his twin did not want to read it. "But we have to, don't we?"

"Yes, Ianto, we must. In case anyone else shows up there. We have to go for them."

"There is no telling what is going to await us there," Ianto said. "I shouldn't, but I hope no one else finds it."

Ianto and Seamus were twenty-six years and three months old when they placed the corded lock and key around their necks.

Chapter Ten
Audrey

Audrey felt the world spinning around her as she hung upside down by a rope and from one foot at nearly the very top of the arena. She had to remember that it was in fact herself that spun, but thinking the opposite made her feel less dizzy. She wondered what it might be like for her so high up, looking down at the thousands of faces in the stands were she acrophobic. She supposed it was probably a very good thing that she wasn't.

Audrey, stop poking and focus, would you?—Aubrey was thinking to her sister, as she spun as well a few feet from her sibling. And she came out of her day-dreamy thoughts for a moment, going back into them at the sight of Aubrey hanging there. They had been in a similar way the day they were born. She knew this by the single time their mother had told them of it. It had been as though the story had made their mother ill, Audrey recalled, the woman's face having been one of extreme disgust in the telling of it. Still, it was tempting to swing over Aubrey's way and get caught up with her and her ropes, re-enacting their birth to see if it would still be and feel the same as it had the first time. She did not do this though, resisting and finishing out their flawless routine. When they were through, they twisted and slithered, shimmied and flipped down the length of rope to the applause, before they bowed together and ran back behind the curtains.

Audrey was ready to finish out the night. She was tired for some reason, and she found it a little worrisome, as she didn't tire easily. She hoped that she was not coming down with any kind of illness. She felt that to be foolish thinking, for she felt fine—just tired. It would pass, she decided. Rest was soon to come and there was little else she could then do about it.

As it usually happened, Audrey would choose someone from the audience to use as her focal point during her routine. This was the twenty-second night in a row that the same person in the designated seat had shown and after that show, he sought Audrey out in her and Aubrey's room. When

Aubrey opened the door at his knocking to find the crystal blue-eyed, blond gentleman at their threshold, she smiled and knew at once that he was there for her sister. She called to her in the usual way and the man smiled back, ever so much more when Audrey came and took Aubrey's place.

"I am sorry to intrude—" he began, his accent making Audrey's bare toes curl.

"No—please, do come in," she invited. "We were just going to have tea. Would you care to join us?"

He accepted graciously and sat at their table, having Earl Grey with no cream or sugar. Their introductions were brief, his mind of definite business and he was not intending to leave until he stated it.

"It is of a sort of delicate nature," he said. Without a word, Aubrey gave a nod to excuse herself and she went into the bedroom, closing the door behind her.

"Delicate," Audrey said then, a little nervous for though she found him to be terribly attractive and his very presence made her young heart flutter, she almost feared whatever it was that he had on his mind.

"As I know you've noticed," he began, "I have been coming here often as of late."

"Yes."

"Audrey—" he said, laying the bait. "I am quite wealthy and I travel the world for a living. I get to see things you probably just get to read about, for I know you do not get to travel, being in this immovable circus."

Audrey's heart was pounding in her chest and it was echoing in Aubrey's. He continued.

"I can tell that you wish to see more of the world. It shows in your eyes each night while you hanging there like the sacrificial lamb—you're so distant in your imagining of far away places. I can give this sort of life to you—do you not see what I am trying to say to you?"

Audrey said nothing still, her eyes on his face, taking it in as she tried to ride the waves of his thoughts, but she could not think straight—he was too beautiful. And then he went in for the kill:

"I want to marry you and take you with me."

From the other room, they heard Aubrey's teacup and saucer clatter to the floor, the spoon making a terrible racket as it too fell with the shattered China. They jumped, as startled by the sound as Audrey's twin had just displayed that she was at the proposal.

Audrey's suitor returned to his question at hand and caressed her delicate white fingers in his. He was smiling at her and his beautiful aqua eyes were pleading to her for a *yes.*

They had, after several years of working at it, mastered their telepathy: Aubrey and Audrey were able to communicate not only with their backs to one another, but as far as in separate rooms. It had seemed invasive to them at first, until they were actually able to do it, and a thought had to be shared before it could be acknowledged. They learned as well to block others out of their thoughts and as the turbaned man had once been able to do, he could no longer pick up on their thoughts and read them. It was a little harder to keep them hidden from the animals, however, and as they could grasp anything and everything anyone was thinking at any given time—if they wanted to—they sometimes did. This did not trouble the twins at all—they knew the animals were better secret-keepers than most humans.

Tell him you'll think on it—Aubrey's words shot into Audrey's mind.

But he has money! He could show me the world—Audrey protested back.

Please, Audrey—tell him to come back! We need to talk about this!

He could see her hesitation.

"I can take you anywhere you like," he was saying. "*Anywhere.* Audrey—" He said at her lowered eyes. "I'll give you anything you want—I adore you—"

Audrey felt a sharp pain in the bottom of her foot and she clenched her teeth against the cry it was causing.

"Are you all right?" he asked, touching her arm. She rose to her feet quickly, pulling away from him, though she hardly wanted to.

"Audrey—"

The sharpness struck her again and she knew Aubrey was dancing across the broken China, even before she heard it crunching under her sister's shoes.

"Can you come back tomorrow?" she forced out. "I-I just want a day. To think on it. You understand? Just one day?"

He stood as well, slowly, his disappointment unmasked. But it was flooded over by his beautiful smile again and tomorrow did not seem so very far away for him. The dashing man took her hands, kissed them both and promised to return the following evening—and every one thereafter until she said yes to his proposal.

Audrey sighed when the door closed, caught between elation and being absolutely crushed.

"He won't give in, Aud," Aubrey said, returning to her sister's side. "Because he's been triggered by hope. And you did that to him—looking at him every night like you do."

"You know I have to do that. It's not my fault he sits in the same seat every single time," Audrey sighed.

"You know that since the very first time you saw him, you've been looking at him for other reasons."

"Really—no matter what you say—I do not know what to do." She flopped down on a plush chair. "He wants to take me traveling, Aub—*traveling*."

"You could travel *now*, if you wanted to."

And this was certainly true: they were free to roam or leave, so long as they gave fair forewarning to their guardian, so their act could be replaced.

"I know this. But he has *money*—"

"What money? There's no telling whether he truly has any money."

"Not without going with him."

"And then it might be too late."

Audrey wanted to cry. She knew he was a stranger to her but that mattered very little when his offers were so great and he was so gloriously handsome.

But she would wait. She would give it until the next day.

But when the next day arrived, Audrey found herself wondering if she should have said yes to the stranger and if she had, would she have met the same fate as he? For when she began her act and scouted for him from her place above the arena, she was horrified to find that he was not in his usual place. She tried to find him from up there, looking for those crystalline eyes—but she could not find him anywhere. She rushed to her quarters after her act to await him, but he did not show.

Every day for the next week, she watched and waited, and hoped, and though she still did not know what she would say to him, Audrey hoped he would come.

61

But he never did.

Aubrey found her sister in a state of turmoil after the second week, when Audrey realized that her suitor was not going to come back. Something had most likely happened to him—something tragic, she thought, for why else after having given her such a promise would he not have come back? At least to beg for her hand one last time. Aubrey could feel the aching in her sister's heart as she held her and comforted her, wishing she would at least cry to let out some of the pain because so long as she did not, it was all the more intense for the both of them. But Audrey's eyes remained dry and she was silent, not knowing what to say about any of it.

At least you are safe—Aubrey thought to her. *It is selfish of me to say so, but I am grateful that you did not go— or else I would be worrying about you just as you are fretting now about him—*

Audrey wrapped her arms about her sister, squeezing her tightly back. She could not argue with that. And that she was concerned for the missing man—she did not have any love for him. How could she? She would not waste another thought or heart beat on the matter of it and instead continued on with her life—with the circus and with her sister, who loved her most of all.

For their constant thirst for knowledge, they also pursued studies in other and quite unorthodox subjects: Aubrey took up a fascination in astroseismology and on clear nights and without a telescope or any other instrument, she would lay in the grassy field outside of the big top and stare into the stars. Mars and Venus were her favorites—the planetary lovers always seeming to be so tragically removed from one another.

To counter this, Audrey lessoned herself in dysteleology and cryptobiology, for though she and her sister both felt that they were now in their natural element, albeit hidden away in a manner of speaking, they had in their previous life been seriously displaced. She thought the subjects to be only rather accurate in reference to themselves. It was to their great advantage that though they studied these subjects separately, it was no matter—whatever one learned, the other inherently knew, without ever cracking open the same books.

They were both very much fanatics of aerophilately, and they had built up quite a collection of stamps for themselves. This was a passion that their fans grew to know and instead of flowers or other traditional gifts, they brought them their stamps. It was no wonder that after years and years of taking these and used postage from discarded envelopes, that they at long last received something stamped of their own.

The girls were just finishing in their dressing for an evening show, months after the incident with the stranger, when the tiny woman in her Spanish dress came hurrying toward them, waving a lavender envelope in the air in one hand and one yellow envelope in the other.

"I forgot to give these to you, my dolls!" she said to them apologetically, looking very much like a doll herself. Her excitement over them was unmasked, for it was very rare that anyone there ever received true mail, let alone anything so elegant as those two letters.

"What ever could those be?" Audrey wondered, taking them both and handing the one addressed to her sister to Aubrey.

"Never mind that—" she smirked. "I hope it isn't junk mail or a trick. That would just be such a shame, such a waste—the envelopes alone are so pretty and I don't feel much like being disappointed today—"

Audrey opened hers first as her sister rambled, thinking for a fleeting second that it might be from the rich stranger whom she had not seen for close to a year now, but instead, she found an invitation inside, accompanied by a small, fancy skeleton key. At that same moment, Aubrey was pulling an ornate lock from her envelope. They held them up together in surprise and amusement, instantly trying them together to see if they fit: They did not.

That is odd—Audrey said of it.

I'll say—Aubrey agreed.

They wanted to remain there and look the little ornaments over and study them more closely, but they had to hurry off to perform their act. It was a futile attempt, for neither of them could hold her focus while in the arena. For the first time in their career with the circus, both of the sisters had accidents while working: Audrey missed her trapeze and as she fell through the air, she caught onto her twin, pulling her from the tightrope that she was traveling across. There was much gasping and many cries from everyone in the big top as

63

they fell from the great height, though thankfully they landed in an awaiting safety net. The ringleader ran to their sides, though their fellow acrobats already there to help them onto solid ground, the fear on his face plain for all to see. The audience applauded loudly when all was found to be well, but to everyone's dismay, they could not finish out the night for their distraction was too great and concentration was found to be impossible for them. They retired to their quarters instead, to stare at the invitations and envelopes, key and lock for the remainder of the night. It did not make sense to them: a key and a lock that did not go together.

What would be the point of that? They were both wondering.

They are invitations—Aubrey was thinking. *Is it possible that other people got them too?*

And maybe they received locks and keys as well? Audrey speculated. *Perhaps it is all part of a game?*

Maybe they're lucky talismans?

Maybe they're not for anything.

Game or not, as much as the two of them loved where they now were in their lives, and for all that they loved what they were spending their time doing, they were both eager to have a change of scenery. It was as the mysteriously missing stranger had claimed of it, and the only unfortunate part of the big top remaining stationary—they did not get to make it out and see the world. Never mind that the world came to them—it was just not the same. There was no argument between them about the invitations: they would leave in one week.

Aubrey and Audrey were twenty-two years and seven months old when they placed the corded lock and key around their necks.

Chapter Eleven
Bonnie

Another night—another nightmare. It never ended and it did not seem like it ever would. Bonnie dreaded going to sleep, she dreaded dreaming. It did not matter how much praying she did and it did not matter that she lived in the convent with the nuns for all of her life but the first week of it. She felt like she was empty in every waking moment, and when she slept, disaster and destruction filled the void. There was never rescuing blackness, but always, always-relentless mayhem. There were many nights that she vowed to stay up to instead sleep during the day. The nuns would of course never allow this. Whether or not Bonnie went to bed at all hours of the night or all hours of the morning, she would still be required to rise at six to do her chores and attend to her studies. It had always been this way and she felt it might always be. For being in such a holy place, she did not believe she could ever be closer to Hell.

This particular night of frightful dreams beheld visions of conjoined kittens, litters upon litters of them, being cut apart from one another and tossed into separate heaps in deep-dug holes in the ground. It was bloody and terrible, and more than she could stand.

Bonnie got out of her little bed and left her simple room, heading bare of foot down the corridors until she found herself in the dark chapel. There was no light but that of the flickering votives in the front left of the room. She went down the aisle through the center of the chapel and stood under the incredible statue of the Virgin Mary that towered over her, nearly touching the ceiling with its bowed head. Of course Bonnie only believed that this monstrous figure was the Holy Mother, as she had been told such since reaching the convent. She never knew this for herself, for the statue was completely enwrapped in an endless bandaging of gauze and dust and cobwebs. Someone's penance, she imagined, having to wrap that thing. Whatever the reason for it, Bonnie could only imagine. But now she was here beneath it, too afraid of her own dreams to be afraid of the fact that it was like a mummy eternally in prayer.

"Please stop the dreams, please stop them tonight!"
she whispered, now on her little nightgown-covered knees.
This was not the first time she had come here to beg at the
Virgin's feet. "And if you cannot stop the dreams, at least help
me know what they are for and what they mean."

Bonnie sighed and though she was full of tears, she
did not shed them—she could not. Bonnie was far too frozen
for that. She looked up from her clenched hands to the votives
where they forever burned. She stood and went to them,
holding her breath so she would not make any of them go out.
She was forbidden to touch them, to light them or to put them
out, but she found comfort in their yellow glow within the red
and blue glass. She wanted to hover her little cold fingers over
the burning flames, grab the searing hot glass to shatter the
endless, repetitive waves of time, but she dared not move any
closer to them. It was mesmerizing though, the dancing of the
fire, but after a few more long moments and not a single
miracle exposed, she headed back to bed. She lay awake for a
very long while, not wanting to go back to sleep, though she
knew she ought to, but it was more than likely—she just
wouldn't. She knew that this was because what she really
wanted was to be held and comforted until the shadowy
remains of her night terrors had passed and it was again safe to
close her eyes. She would not get that here at the convent—
certainly not from the cold and seemingly soulless nuns, and
Bonnie knew this. She was surrounded by women who had not
one caring or maternal thread in their body—not for anyone
but their God, and certainly not for a misfit little girl with no
past. They never expressed affection of any kind and they
never gave sentiments of it either. Bonnie had never been
touched by a single one of them in a loving manner, and if she
could not expect that from them, she wondered if she would
ever get that from anyone, anywhere in the entire world. It did
not seem so—at least not in *her* world.

Bonnie hoped that she would not grow to be heartless
and empty. She did not want to become a lifeless figure in a
hollow habit, with no light shining in her heart or her eyes. Or
worse still: a frozen-stiff, forever-praying statue of herself.

But then something different from the usual was
happening, and as it was the first of many surprising things
that would happen to her: it gave her hope. She began to
expect it, to need it.

Bonnie was through fighting the onset of returning sleep, despite that she was terrified to give in, but as colors were beginning to swirl through the blackness in her mind, she suddenly became overwhelmed with a sense of complete comfort and protection. She wondered if the Blessed Mother was visiting her finally. But it was something closer to her, something in her heart that was warming and it was as though a missing entity was now there and embracing her. She felt her breath catch and she lay very still, holding onto the feeling for as long as she could, holding onto her consciousness for as long as she was able in order to keep the warmth. She would hold her very life's breath if she thought it would help it to stay. But Bonnie drifted then and the nightmares did not return that night.

When she awoke in the morning, the convent was gone, her little closet of a room had been replaced with a garret of crystal clarity and though the sky was filled with clouds of gray iron and the rain beat down on the clear panes, she sighed with relief and gave appreciative thanks that the entire flashback was only that.

Her Beau had known that she would just be waking, and he had entered her room just as Bonnie was sitting up. She greeted him with a relieved smile and offered outstretched arms, to which he happily took. He sat beside her on the bed when he realized that she was trying to catch her breath and she did not immediately let go of him.

"More dreams?" he asked knowingly, pushing her sleep-tousled hair from her face.

"More."

Beau sighed with concern. It had been more than twenty years since he had found her, and while the dreams masked as nightmares had been coming at an incredible rate in the beginning, they had eventually tapered off and were only occasional. Until recently.

"I will not let you be taken from me again, Bonnie," he promised once more, for the thousandth time, pressing his forehead to hers. "And you're never going back to that wretched convent either."

"Am I never going to get over that?" she wondered aloud.

"You will when you let it go," he assured her.

"But you can't stop it if it's going to happen," she insisted.

"Why do you say that, love?" Beau asked, hurting at the thought just as she did.

"Because some day—" She could not finish and he knew what she meant.

"Not by desertion or *death* will I ever leave you or lose you again." He cradled her head and their eyes connected with a depth that they would never have with anyone else.

"If you go, I don't want to stay," she whispered and they both felt the painful knot that such a thought caused.

"*Not, ever,*" Beau insisted.

It was moments later, but Bonnie smiled finally and laughed. It was deceiving—he knew that she still hurt inside. Still, Bonnie took her brother's face in her hands to give his mouth a kiss, and then she sighed. A battle of fears won: if only for the moment.

Beau's thoughts interrupted her own.

"Do you think other twins get on as we do?" he asked, the tingling effect of her kiss on his lips still lingering. This brought Bonnie to grin.

"You mean intimately so?" she teased.

"Exactly so."

"I think people probably think things of us that aren't at all true. Besides, what does that matter when *I* know you prefer the company of—" She searched for a tactful way to put her statement. "—*others*. Was that from all of your years with the monks?" she questioned, wondering why she had never thought to ask him that before.

"Not in the way *you* think, you dirty girl," he clarified. "I was never mistreated here. In fact, I was very *well* treated and cared for. Maybe that is why I have my preferences. I did enjoy their company." He grinned, seeing her brows rise in mock teasing. "*Only* their company, Bonnie."

Bonnie smiled softly then, her heart warming that her brother was so happy and that they were so fortunate to have one another. He smiled back and ran his hand through her hair and pulled her close again.

"And yours, of course," he added. She put her forehead against his, both of them smiling and squinting because they were too close to see one another properly, their eyes merging into one. Bonnie laughed.

"I love you, Beau," she said, musing. His grin softened and he held her head, still pressed to him. He thought for a moment and then finally spoke.

"I feel more for you than I could ever express by saying *that* to you," he nearly whispered. Bonnie felt her heart warm more at that sentiment and she wrapped her arms about his neck to hug him close.

"Oh Beau—" She sighed.

She felt that she could simply melt right into him and when he pulled away enough to take her face in his hands to kiss her as she just had him, Bonnie wondered how she would ever find someone as perfect as Beau was to her—or who could be as loving. It was a battle she fought constantly, and a forbidden argument she found herself having inside her very soul each and every time she let any other man touch or kiss her. Never could anyone compare it seemed, and she knew it was the same for him. Still, she would never deny him his heart or his needs of others, just as he would not deny it of her—no matter that a fulfilling encounter was uncommon for either of them. She took comfort in knowing that it would always be for them just as he had said—beyond their siblinghood. Beyond even love.

It was afternoon when Bonnie arrived back home. She burst through the door, eager to see Beau for the first time that day, as he had been away for two weeks exhibiting his art abroad, and had now just come back home. But she halted at the sight of the mail piled up on the floor under the slot in their front door. She threw the garbage mail onto a table and picked out two interesting looking envelops—one gold and addressed to Beau and the other one a pale spring green that was intended for her. Beau was just coming down the stairs when he saw her standing in the hall where she was studying the lettering on each envelope. Other than their names, they were exactly alike.

"Bonnie! I didn't know the mail had come," he said. She did not immediately respond. "What do you have there, love?" he asked, his smile dimming at seeing her grown serious by the sight of her drawn brow. He kissed her there as she handed Beau his envelope, while she still looked hers over. He took and opened his, a lock on a black cord falling onto the floor with a resounding ping. Bonnie bent down to pick it up while Beau read the simple instructions on the enclosed card. His expression had become far too solemn for Bonnie's liking and she hurriedly opened her envelope as well, a key falling out into her hand.

"That is interesting," she said. She held them up together, the skeleton key and lock being completely unmatching from one another. She handed Beau's back to him and grinned at him. He didn't smile back with as much mirth as he had only moments before.

"What's wrong? What's on the card?" she was asking. She took his card and read it and then quickly pulled hers out of its envelope to see that it was the same missive. She looked at him after reading it, Beau waiting to see what she had to say about it.

"It's for tomorrow night," she said.

"I know."

"Isn't that somewhere near where Stonehenge used to be?" Bonnie asked, her stomach beginning to feel a little funny.

"Yes."

"Is there any way we can even get there that fast?" she wondered.

"We could."

"Should we even go?" she asked after a pause and Beau searched her eyes for a moment.

"I think we should." But Bonnie was not convinced that he truly thought it best and certainly she was a bit leery of it. They usually loved parties and gatherings, being frequent hosts of them themselves, and it was but for the warning on the invite that made them feel as they did. But her brother had never steered them wrong—certainly he had not made any harmful decisions for them yet, neither of them had, and so she trusted him as she always did.

"Maybe it isn't as serious as it comes off," Bonnie suggested, but somehow she knew it was more than the words on the paper could portray. They both knew this.

The rest of their day passed in quiet contemplation, each of them off in their own rooms with their own thoughts and nothing that they had had planned for the evening came to any sort of culmination. It was very late into the night before Bonnie felt that she could finally try to sleep. But she found that she could only lie there in restlessness and she could not calm her thoughts enough for respite. What seemed to be hours passed as she thought obsessively of the mystery of the invitations. It became much too overwhelming for everything else refused to come to mind but that, and it began to pain her head—it was maddening and she did not want to think about them for a second longer. Certainly, she thought, not by herself.

Bonnie gave in at last with a frustrated sigh, and got out of bed. She hated that she felt imposing whenever she sought out her twin in the night, but she knew that he was alone this night. Of course, even if he had not been, she knew that Beau would never refuse her. Time and again he had proven this to her. She tiptoed through the dark halls and up the steps to Beau's room at the top of the monastery. She found him lying on his bed in flame light with music filtering into his ears through his headphones. His eyes were closed though she knew he too was awake, and Beau had known she would come to him eventually that night. He felt her standing above him and opened his eyes, smiling warmly, invitingly at her. Bonnie smiled back and went to his offered up hand, before he sat up to put out the candles beside his bed. She burrowed in close to him when they both lay down and he moved one of the two tiny speakers so it was in her ear and the other still in his. Bonnie sighed, her head on his chest as they absorbed the ambient sounds, and he kissed the top of her head, holding her close.

Despite being comforted by one another and their needing the rest, they were to get very little sleep that night. Morning seemed to come far too quickly for them both and though they desired to remain where they were in Beau's bed for the entire day rather than face whatever lay ahead, they took to a usual routine, and packed what they felt they would need for their journey. It was too soon that the time for leaving came.

"I don't want to go, Beau," she said at the door, stepping too close for him to open it. He turned to her and lowered his face near hers.

"I know, love. Neither do I," he responded softly. She chewed her lip for a second, thinking out the words before she spoke them.

"So why are we doing this?" she asked, and though neither of them had the answer, neither of them could think of a good enough reason to avoid it.

"I don't know what we're going to or what we're going to find there—I just don't want things to change," Bonnie began. "I don't want anything to be different."

He smiled and rubbed her cheek.

"It won't be. Why ever would it?"

"I don't know. I just feel something." He kissed her forehead, knowing what she meant by it.

"Well love, at least there is this: if the world as we know it does change, *our* world won't—because we will not let it." He grinned at her then. "Of course, there's always a chance that it could get even *better*. Right?"

Beau and Bonnie were thirty-five years and three months old when they placed the corded key and lock around their necks.

Chapter Twelve
Gabriel

The day that finally arrived for Gabriel and his twin, though expected, had felt eluding up until the very moment that it happened. Their parents had had quite enough of their children fighting and bickering and at just the age of sixteen and after one too many close calls that could have cost either twin their young life, their mother and father decided that enough was enough. No matter their separation—beyond beds and beyond rooms, they needed to be completely and residentially separated for their own good. This meant that they were being made to move on and it required that they both go into the world and make their own money to help survive. Gabriel had not a quandary with this, for he had spent much of his time looking for just the perfect place to go and live and just the perfect place to work in. It so happened that Gabriel had a pension for working with numbers and so much so that he had made his own teachers' heads spin. And so with a fistful of letters of recommendation, all of his worldly possessions and a fresh, new black and blue right eye (compliments of his sister who had broken their prior treaty in exchange for his harassment of her) he set out to his new life, his mother in tow. He saw to it that he made immediate success of himself and was able to set her up in a place of her own, where their father could be with her and they could stop sacrificing their marriage in the name of saving the twins from complete ruin.

The building that served as Gabriel's workplace was also his home. It was a skyscraper of magnificent proportions. It was made of brass and copper that would remain forever shining and never take on a patina. The windows were thick and tall and narrow, and they bubbled out between the metal skeleton of the walls. The floors were very thick, scratch-resistant glass and between the unbreakable panes of it were never-stopping cogs and gears. The constant motion of people walking on them was enough to jar the gears to keep them moving and in turn, this kept the electricity running. In the evenings and throughout the night, there was enough of a

73

reserve that any needed light or power could be used without fail.

Gabriel found this to be a most welcome and perfect change. It was exactly how he had wanted it to be. His home was his haven and he loved it. His job of crunching digits and twisting equations was his life's work and when his head hit the pillow every night, never did his existence feel unfulfilled. He could not have chosen a more perfect path. He could not have been placed in better circumstances. There was nothing that could alter that for him—except when he was to travel.

It was by train that Gabriel had to make his first journey away. He was to voyage through several countries and in two days' time, meet his destination, shake hands, work some figures, shake hands again on a nice accord, and then return home. Simply enough, this was not to happen for him without one very large snag.

When he reached the station and awaited his train on the platform with his plaid suitcase in hand, a strange pang hit his belly. Whether it was discord or delight, he could not tell, for the sensation was so very close to both. But when the train finally arrived and he boarded and opened the door to his cabin, he knew exactly what the sensations were all for.

"Oh. *You.*"

From where she had been sitting, Georgina sat up on her bunk and after narrowing her eyes at recognizing her brother standing there, she hurled the book in her hands at him.

"What are *you* doing here?" she asked as he entered the little room and shoved her belongings off of the second bunk.

"It appears, that this is my cabin too, wench."

"Oh, *no it is not!*" she argued. "This is *my* cabin, you ugly wretch and *you* can't stay here!"

"I love that you call me ugly when we're *twins!*"

"Small technicality. You still need to leave."

"Well I suggest that you go and find someone to straighten it out then." He threw her book back at her.

"Why don't *you* go and find someone?"

"Because I'll happily stay here and torture you," he said with nonchalance, though it made his very nerves grate to think of it.

Georgina stood in a huff and left him there, only to return a few minutes later with the car attendant and some unfortunate news.

"This here is the only cabin left," she said to her brother. And then she looked at the wary attendant and with all sweetness to him continued. "Is there nothing else that can be arranged? Because if I must stay in here with this ridiculous and hideous brat that he is, we *will* kill each other before the trip is over."

"She's telling you the truth," Gabriel said. "Though she's usually full of lies. I'll probably throw her off of this train during the night."

"Not if I find a way to smother the life out of you first, of course." She grinned mockingly.

The attendant was unsure as to how to take their comments and found it best to back away slowly and offer no unwanted advice.

"You're so good at nothing," Georgina praised, shoving her way back into the cabin and moving her things out of Gabriel's reach.

"I see you've become more—thriving since I've been away," he said sarcastically. "Traveling now and such."

"You being away—far away—would improve anyone's lot in life. And yes, I own an animal rescue farm. Kind of like a sanctuary."

"Well, certainly that explains the smell," Gabriel quipped, though he could really smell nothing but the gardenias that his sister had in her hair.

The entire train ride resulted in one continuous squabble, even as they left the car to dine, Gabriel flaunting his rare steak in front of her as he savored it with exaggeration and she reprimanded and scolded him for his insensitivity.

"Do you have no blood in your veins?" she accused.

"Plenty," he admitted, pointing his dripping knife at her to indicate such before licking it. "Probably more than you—you have to have meat in your diet for that! Here—" He shoved his salad plate across the table to her with his fork as though the thought of touching it was as equally unappetizing to him as his eating meat was to her. "Have some more rabbit food. What do you suppose they meant when they said, "the rabbit died"? Be the rabbit, George and let's see how we can make that happen."

"You're an idiot."

"And you have nothing more intelligent to say back? I guess *you're* an idiot."

"Honestly, Gabe—"

"Yes, I am being honest." He grinned at her sardonically. She narrowed her eyes at him, her appetite completely gone. She picked up his glass of red wine and then threw it in his face, the burgundy soaking into and staining his white shirt at once. He froze, her movements having happened so fast.

"Oh here, this will take out that nasty stain—" And she threw her glass of club soda in his face as well, before she stood and sauntered out of the dining car, sprinting once she'd gotten through the door. She reached the cabin before he did, though he had sprung up and run after her, and she succeeded in locking him out. For the entire night.

And so their trip of only a few days of one another's torturous company felt to be stretched out to more like a few weeks, and the return trip found them not to be spared of one another's companionship either. It did not matter that in an effort to avoid one another on the train back, they had both coincidentally rerouted new tickets on a new day—again for one another's same train, same time and same cabin.

Like a pair of divergent magnets they would seem to be continuously drawn together and thrown into inescapable situations with one another. In the months that followed their first meeting, a new and unwelcome pattern ensued. When Gabriel booked passage on a ship, Georgina was suddenly with him, and there too the cabins were overbooked. As they were both too stubborn to give up the small cabin they did have, they suffered it out. The following year, Gabriel was scheduled to go into Egypt, where his only means of travel were by camelback. It was their reoccurring luck with one another that only one camel was available for riding and as neither of them was willing to budge on this either, they had to ride on it together. The journey resulted in bruises and bite marks, red skin burns and a fat lip. And none of it, of course was attributed to the laboring beast.

Gabriel was in a state of unrest when his travel continued and his sister did not cease in showing up in the same places. Unplanned and uncalculated—and unavoidable. Never for them, was there an alternative place to be and spite and ire sparked like flame for the duration of their company together, no matter their circumstances. It was an unintentional coincidence, a curse—a trick that they were presented with so often that they should have become used to it, though they never quite managed to.

It only seemed natural that they both received an invitation on the same day, their violet and black envelopes containing a key for Gabriel and a lock for Georgina, bidding their arrival in two days hence, to the listed address.

"Are you stalking me?" Georgina asked him as they stood together on an airfield awaiting the only available biplane to their matching destination, and it was pointless in answering her. His question would have been the same for her.

"I am actually a little surprised to see you here, George," Gabe said, "seeing as you only have cloven animals in your sanctuary—I'd think you would have stuck to ground travel."

"It happens to be the fastest way to get there, imbecile, and no one would know cloven animals better than you."

At this, their plane arrived and Gabriel called *shotgun* for the front seat.

"If only I had one," Georgina muttered before giving her brother a red, if-looks-could-kill smile.

Georgina and Gabriel were thirty years and eight months old when they put the corded lock and key around their necks.

Chapter Thirteen
The Labyrinth Project

It was ten-thirty when Ianto and Seamus reached their destination. They had chosen to drive there, and though they had left in plenty of time to get there before eleven-thirty, they grew nervous at being as late as they were. As it was, Aubrey and Audrey were there already, both of them standing at the mouth of the labyrinth, brushing some wild ivy from a plaque that they had found by its doorway. They saw the newly arrived twins approaching and both of them brushed their mussed hands on their white lawn dresses in unison. Seamus and Ianto exchanged a glance at how uncanny their identicallity was, their movements as well as their appearances—the two of them looking like two grown up little girls with simple white bows pulling back their hair. But they also took note that one of them was wearing white tights and white Mary Jane shoes while the other was completely barefoot. They made their introductions, brief and nervous, the girls pulling the ivy back again to show the boys the sign.

CROSS THE THRESHOLD WITH CARE
ENTER THIS WORLD, IF YOU DARE
ONE WITHOUT THE OTHER, BOTH ARE LACK
REUNITE OR NEVER COME BACK

"A little grim sounding," Audrey said in its regard. As it was exactly as Seamus and Ianto would have had it—as it was in their stolen plans for the maze, they could only nod solemnly.

They said very little else short of small talk, the other two pair of twins showing in a short amount of time following the first two.

Bonnie and Beau arrived next, both of them looking eager but appropriately apprehensive. They did little more than introduce themselves and shake hands with the others. Georgina and Gabriel appeared moments later, both elegantly dressed and arguing as usual, but they reigned themselves in enough to hold polite conversation with those who awaited them.

"So, what do we do now?" Georgina asked. Those who knew the answer were hesitant to respond but Seamus was the first to brave saying something.

"Do any of you know why you're here?" he asked. Everyone shook his or her head.

"Not a clue," Gabriel said. "And as much as I hate to admit it, it's the first thing I think George and I have ever agreed on in our lives."

"Probably the last," Georgina concurred.

"You have likely noticed that you each received a lock or key—" Ianto continued for his brother. Everyone nodded to that. "And that, although they probably arrived together, none of them fit with one another."

"You seem to know a lot more about all of this than any of the rest of us," Bonnie said, taking a hold of the key that Seamus dangled to look at it in the moonlight and to compare it to the one she had: it looked nothing like hers.

"There is a reason for that," Seamus admitted, addressing both her spoken and unspoken thoughts.

"I want to know why *we* are here," Georgina said. "Why me and Gabe? Why you? And you?" She nodded to Audrey and Beau and their sisters. "Why *you* two?" she asked of Ianto and Seamus. "And why only the eight of us? I can see by you two—" And she looked at the blond girls. "That this must have something to do with twins. Gabe and I are twins as well, and so the rest of you must be."

"That is right," Aubrey said. "It does have to do with us all being twins—" She showed them the plate on the wall.

"Well that is disconcerting," Georgina said.

"A bit," Ianto agreed.

"What does being here in nearly the middle of the night have to do with it?" Bonnie asked, though aside from Beau, she probably knew best of the mystic pull the area they were in contained.

"We all have to be on the other side of that wall by midnight," Ianto explained.

"But why?" Aubrey asked. "What difference does the time make?"

"It is a little complicated," Ianto began.

"Try us," Gabriel said.

Ianto sighed, still hardly believing himself that they were there.

"This is a labyrinth. Its entry is like a porthole and it closes at one minute past twelve."

"Aside from that sounding completely unbelievable, what if we choose not to go in?" asked Gabriel.

"You are already in," Seamus said.

For a moment, no one believed that of him and no one moved, but when nothing more was said, Bonnie left Beau's side to try to step away from the wall. In the dim light, another wall had encircled where they stood, engulfing them all within it, but for an archway leading into a corridor where a few doors were visible.

"This is impossible," she breathed, and yet it was true. The others followed her to it, scaling a few feet down in each direction, and finding that there was no way out.

"This is *insane*," Georgina said.

They returned to circle around the two brothers.

"You still never said why *us*," Beau pointed out. "Of all of the many twins in the world, and I'm sure there are thousands—hundreds of thousands—it's down to the *eight* of us."

Ianto and Seamus exchanged a look, Ianto shrugging at the possibility of things. Truly all they had were hunches and speculations.

"It is probably safe to say that you all live in a rather—unique, kind of place," he began. "A sky-scraping tower, a big top that looks like a paper-cut, maybe—?"

"What about a sanctuary?" Georgina asked, sounding partially jesting though she certainly did not feel as though she were. "Made up of a million interlocking pieces?"

"*That, exactly.*"

"How do you know this?" Aubrey asked. "You sent the invitations--?"

"No, we didn't," Seamus insisted. "We're not sure who sent them—we got them too. But we did design those places that you know. And that has something to do with the reason we are all here."

"Wait—" Beau interrupted. "You two designed the monastery that I grew up in? The place that Bonnie and I now live in?"

"Yes," Ianto said, wondering why he felt guilt when at that moment he should have felt proud at their accomplishments.

"And the opera house that Bonnie works in—but that place is ancient!"

"We created that too," Seamus admitted. "It was our first project, actually."

"How old are you, anyway?" Bonnie added, thinking them to look rather young. "Beau and I are older than you two, we've got to be—how is that possible? Even if we were the same age as you—Beau's been at the monastery since he was an infant. The opera house has been a part of my life always. When did you start these places?"

"We were still teens when we started," Seamus explained.

"Even still," Georgina began, not letting them explain. "Gabe started working in your *Tower* years ago and *that* isn't even possible. In fact there is no way that it could be! Either you're a lot older than us—*doubtful*—or we're a lot younger than you."

"Doubtful too, on George's account," Gabriel said.

"Shut up," she answered back.

"And you've made this too," Aubrey said, referring to the maze. "And our home, at the circus—that incredible model was your doing?"

"Well, not exactly," Seamus began. "We only designed them all. And this one—well, mostly."

"What does that mean? *Mostly?*" Georgina inquired cautiously.

"What it means is that we never finished it," Ianto said, his apprehensions rising. "And the original idea of it was for the maze to be a soul-searching kind of place."

"Like a meditation labyrinth," Beau said, a bit of relief setting in.

"Like a searching for your *soul*, sort of labyrinth," Seamus corrected.

"Well isn't that the same thing?" Gabriel asked.

"No, it's not the same," Bonnie answered for the brothers. She turned to Beau and grasped his hand tightly, and in return his arm went around her shoulders. They knew exactly what it meant. "It's a test of sorts. That is why *twins* were chosen: to test our bonds." She leaned her forehead on her brother's chest then, the realization of her own words coming clear to her. "Not again, Beau," she whispered.

From the dark shadows that crossed in their eyes and their following embrace, the others knew at the very least what the search would entail.

"We are going to be parted from our twin, aren't we?" Audrey concluded.

"Yes," Ianto confirmed. "That is exactly right. But I'm not sure for how long. And getting back to one another— it isn't going to be an easy search, I'm thinking. It was in our plans to have made it more of a game, had Seamus and I finished it, with multiple ways to get out, if you wanted to just quit. It was supposed to just be a bit of fun. That was our hope for it—to have it be just a simple kind of hide and seek that involved solving puzzles, and exploring your bonds with your soul mate. And that it is meant for twins—that was just an intricate detail, but—"

"But we didn't complete the plans. They were stolen from us and we have no idea by whom," Seamus said. "And so there is no telling what we are going to find in here."

"As long as we find one another by the end, that is all that matters," Aubrey said. "Right? That seems like a simple enough objective."

"Oh, so losing the game would be in *our* best interest," Georgina said, looking at her brother and smirking when he stuck his tongue out at her.

"No--!" Ianto interjected, a small panic rising. "If you don't find each other—well, if I'm thinking that they made this what I think they did—"

"*You* end," Seamus finished. "Your twin ends, your souls—they both end."

"Oh, *great* game!" Georgina said with heavily laced cynicism. And then after a moment, "You are totally serious about all of this—this is for *real* and we're basically trapped in here until we go through and finish the maze?"

"That is about the size of it, yes," Ianto concurred. He attempted a wry smile. "It's that proverbial not letting yourself be defeated or you will be—in all ways."

"Like that cliché trash about how if you die in a dream, you die in life?" Georgina scoffed. "I'm sorry, but that is ridiculous. And impossible."

"We don't know if that would really happen," Seamus defended.

"But why take chances, is what they mean, George," Gabe added.

82

"Whatever."

"I've died in a dream before," Bonnie said softly. And all eyes were on her. "I was torn apart by a polar bear." She said this so matter of factly; no one knew what to say. "Shredded."

"No one is going to die in this place," Beau said, though he could not be sure, and he held Bonnie more tightly to him. No one could know for sure.

"So why the caution then?" Audrey asked.

"Caution is always good," Bonnie endorsed. "But—I didn't die from the dream, you can see that."

"You're linked to your sibling," Aubrey offered to Georgina, wanting to shift the subject. "We all are. That is what they say about us twins, isn't it? That we feel each other's pain and know what the other knows? At least that is how it is for Audrey and I."

Beau nodded in agreement, as it was that way for him and Bonnie as well.

"I think I would have blown my brains out long ago if that were the case for us," Gabriel said in reference to Georgina. "Bad enough I have to know her at all."

"Yes, drop dead please," Georgina said to her brother.

Bonnie buried her face against Beau's chest again and his arms tightened around her even more until he wondered if he would squeeze the life out of her, both of them dreading what was coming.

"Well, that is one of the little things that is supposed to help in solving the maze," Seamus said. "Our ability to help one another, without being together. A little on the experimental side of things, but I suppose it is what gives it some of its personality."

"Are there any other tricks that we should know about this place?" Beau asked. "Any hints or tips you want to give us? What to do, what not to do? It's obvious that we don't get to go in together."

"Don't lose the person you're paired up with," Ianto said, looking long and hard at the lock on the cord around his neck before he looked at Beau. "You both have to be there at the end because you're going to have to open the door to go out, just like you will to get in."

"And just how exactly would we lose whomever we're with?" Aubrey asked, feeling her blood chill at the many possibilities.

"Just don't," Ianto warned. "Our original design had pitfalls just like any other maze but it was supposed to be solvable, truly. Just on the fact that twins—the coincidence that all of you, ended up in our creations—it's enough for me to have some reservations about the reality and non-reality of all of this. And, since we don't know who finished this, or who built it even—"

"We have no idea what will happen in there," Seamus confessed. "Losing your companion could have a domino effect that we don't want to risk."

"How much time do we have to get through it?" Bonnie asked, not yet leaving Beau's arms.

"The good news is that we theorize that there is some kind of a time limit," Seamus said.

"And the bad news?" Georgina asked. "Because there is always bad news too."

"We don't know the bad news," said Ianto.

"*That* is certainly bad enough news," Audrey said.

Bonnie pulled from Beau and looked at him for a long moment, memorizing his face as she so often did.

"Now the returning dreams make sense," Beau said to her softly, cradling her head.

"I wish they would have just gone away," she whispered.

"After this, I think that they will," he assured her. "We've survived this sort of thing before—we will again." He kissed her forehead, tipped up her head and kissed her mouth and then embraced her one last time. "Remember, Bonnie—*better than ever.*"

Aubrey touched Bonnie on the arm gently to interrupt them.

"Maybe we should get going," she suggested, wanting to get through the maze and hating the idea of going into it and its uncertainty as much as Bonnie and Beau and the others did. She returned to Audrey and they gave one another a quick squeeze.

"Give me a hug, harpy," Gabriel said mockingly to Georgina, his arms wide to accept her.

"Oh please, get away you twit," she refused him, sticking her arms out to keep him away.

84

"Just keep your companion near you," Seamus said. "No matter what happens—do not lose sight of each other and keep focused on getting back out."

"Do you expect that we're going to be distracted in there?" Gabriel asked.

"It is more than possible," Seamus said. "I guarantee this maze is unlike anything you may be expecting. So please—the sooner you get out, the better."

A silent moment passed as they prepared themselves as well as they could.

"Everyone have your key or lock?" Ianto asked. They all pulled them off over their heads, and then followed him through the archway to four awaiting, locked doors. They went to the first of them in turn to test their locks and then keys.

In the first door, it was Aubrey's lock that fit. The key holders were hesitant to try but at last, Gabriel's was the one to fit. The door swung open and with a cautious look back at the others, they linked arms and went through, the door closing behind them. In a blink, it seemed to disappear into the wall and left no trace that there had ever before been a door there. This left them all feeling a bit uneasy, but with two of them now in the interworkings of the maze, there was no turning back.

In the second door, it was Seamus's key that took Georgina's lock. They too surrendered to their awaiting entrance, Seamus only looking back once to see his brother nodding at him encouragingly.

Bonnie resisted when the remaining four of them went to the next door, her heart pounding so hard that it seemed to freeze everything within her, even the tears brimming on her lashes.

Ianto's lock fit the door and neither Beau nor Audrey had the key. They looked expectantly at Bonnie. She was able to move then as they stilled, and Ianto gave her a sympathetic half smile and held his hand out to her. She took it trustingly and after the turn of her key had made a most decisive click, they stepped just onto the threshold. Bonnie could not stand to look back at Beau though she knew that he was just at the doorway behind her. She felt Ianto turning back.

"You take care of her," Beau demanded quietly of the man at his sister's side. Bonnie could hear that he was trying to keep his voice strong, but even Beau had a little fear in his tone.

"I will," promised Ianto, his hand squeezing hers reassuringly. "You have my word on that."

Bonnie closed her eyes and as Ianto put his arm around her shoulders, she held her breath as they stepped in and the door closed tightly.

Only Beau and Audrey remained, both of them looking at their lock and key and turning them over in their hands. They said nothing, for what was there to say now? And they went to the last door, Audrey's key, Beau's lock, before they too joined the maze.

Chapter Fourteen
Aubrey and Gabriel

When the door closed behind them, Aubrey and Gabriel found themselves standing in the dark. Neither of them said anything for a moment, until Gabriel suddenly started to laugh.

"What is so funny?" Aubrey asked, turning her head toward him, though she still could not see him.

"Not a thing," he said, trying to stifle his meaningless mirth.

"Oh."

"*Now* what are we supposed to do?" he wondered out loud.

"Should we start walking or something?"

"What? And step into who-knows-what or off of a cliff or something?"

Aubrey did not quite know what to say to that. When Gabriel was able to settle his laughing, he retained a bit of seriousness for her sake.

"Wait, hold on—" He rustled around in his jacket pocket and found his chrome lighter. Aubrey could hear him flip it open but when he went to try to light it, she heard it spring from his hand and it landed somewhere on the ground. She giggled a little bit but put her hand over her mouth to muffle it, not wanting him to take offense.

"Well this is fantastic, isn't it?" Gabriel said with his voice still edged with amusement.

"Come on, let's try to find it," Aubrey suggested, carefully getting onto her hands and knees. She noticed at once that the ground was covered with thick damp moss and it was a fresh bark smell that surrounded them. Gabriel knelt down beside her.

"The ground feels a bit odd, doesn't it?"

"I think we're still outside," Aubrey said in discovery, and as the words came suggestively from her lips, the darkness began to lift ever so slightly.

"But we walked into a room," Gabriel differed. "Didn't we?"

"We walked through a doorway into the dark," she corrected. "Don't you smell the trees and the pine?" Gabriel sniffed the air soundly.

"Sort of—" But he was not certain that he really did. As their surroundings seemed to lighten more for Aubrey, they remained dark to Gabriel.

"We are outside," she said softly. "We're in a forest."

She reached out to touch a fallen tree just in front of them, the bark feeling quite rough and real to her fingertips. When she looked up, it was clearly taller than they were and it seemed to stretch out for a great distance to either side of them, but there was just enough room for them to crawl beneath it.

"Get all the way down and follow me," she said to her companion, before she lay down on her stomach to begin inching under it.

"Where are we going?" he asked though he followed her lead.

"There's an enormous fallen tree. We have to go underneath it," she explained as she was already doing so through the mud and pine needles. "Can you see anything yet?" she asked him once they were under the log.

"Not yet."

"Maybe you have to try harder. Just imagine what the trees look like."

To this, Gabe scoffed.

"Darling, I have lived and worked in a building of metal and glass for nearly the last two-some decades. There are no trees there."

"But surely you have *seen* one before," she insisted.

"Nope."

Aubrey stopped crawling and turned her head back to him over her shoulder.

"What's the matter?" he asked, sensing her stopping.

"I hope you're joking."

"Of course I am." He smiled, feeling around for her. She moved her foot so his hand could grasp her now-muddied white-stockinged ankle. "How much farther do we have to go?"

"We're about half way now."

"Hm. Rather large tree," he deduced. And then he added after a pause, "I sure hope it doesn't fall on us."

"Please just keep going," Aubrey groaned, wanting to kick his hand off of her foot for the comment, but she did not.

They remained silent for the rest of the way, Aubrey helping him to stand up once they were out from under the giant cedar. Gabriel picked at the front of his shirt, which like the rest of him and Aubrey alike, was covered with mud.

"I feel a little messy," he stated.

"You are a sight," Aubrey began. She gasped when he looked up at her.

"What now?" he asked. She reached out to his face and turned it toward the sun that now filtered in through the leafy branches of the trees. She could see him fully as she had before they'd gone into the maze. His eyes were covered over with white as though he'd gone double cataract.

"What, woman? What's the matter?" His hand covered over hers, still against his face.

"You need to try a lot harder to see where you are," she insisted firmly. "Trust me on that."

Gabriel gave half a huff and switched his weight from one foot to the other. He still saw nothing and the white clouds over his eyes grew thicker. He did not notice but she did.

"Gabriel!" He started at her sudden shouting and when he still did not progress, she pulled him to a standing tree and put his hands on it.

"Are you putting my hands on you?" he asked with a mischievous tone.

"Don't be silly. You are touching a tree, which is miles high and bigger around than you and I could reach together," she described.

She could see his frustration beginning to set in when still he felt nothing. She took his hand and put it on her cheek, keeping the other on the tree. He noticed the difference and it was as though a shade of the veil had lifted—he could see shadows from her form and the trees around them, and his eyes became a smoky green.

"Here—" Aubrey pulled him close for him to inhale the scent of her: violets.

"Mm. That's pleasant," he stated, before he reached out to grasp a nearby branch and he took a deep breath of it.

His eyes cleared instantly and it left them a lucid and engaging emerald.

"Whoa—" He looked around, turning in a circle before he ran to the fallen tree. He was not tall enough to see over it. He dropped down to try to see beneath the tree but the distance they had crawled was too far for him to tell where they had come from. He stood then and went back to Aubrey.

"This is rather strange, isn't it?" he said to her. She nodded in complete agreement. He noticed how soiled her dress was then.

"Sorry about that—" and he nodded to the drying mud.

"Yes, well." She absently brushed at it but her thoughts were not on her dress. "We'd better keep going."

Gabriel certainly agreed, though to him it seemed that they were just in a forest and not any sort of maze or puzzle.

"This is going to be impossible," he said pessimistically. Aubrey smirked, as she was usually rather negative herself. For some reason, she wasn't this time.

"We just need to know what to look for," she said, pulling on his arm so he would follow her.

"Like what?"

"Like, I don't know. Pictures in the wood of the trees, or pathways or something," she suggested.

"Did you notice anything odd about this place?" Gabe asked her as they wandered along the rows and rows of trunks and stumps.

"Like what, besides everything?" she teased.

"Like that it was pretty close to midnight when we took that door in here and now it's broad daylight. Like *that* kind of odd."

Aubrey paused and looked around just a bit, as she was a little afraid to really look around just then, for fear that she might see *too much*.

"Unsettling, isn't it?" Gabriel said. She swallowed nervously and nodded at him.

"Definitely."

"I suppose we could look at it this way—"

"What way is that?"

"Well, it's like this place has no rules. And you know what is the best thing about no rules is? It means *no rules*."

"Yes. Well, you know what usually happens when there are no rules: that is when you need them most."

They went on, the trees seemingly never ending. It was this thought that crossed Gabriel's mind when he suddenly began to notice that there really were images in the patterns of the tree bark. He stopped Aubrey, his hand on her arm and when she took a look at what he was seeing, she had to tip her head just slightly to make anything of it.

"Pictures, you said—" Gabriel pronounced to her. She nodded and then pointed to the outline darker than the rest.

"How about that shape there?" she said. "A horse, maybe?"

Gabriel saw something, but he was not sure that it was a horse.

"Are you sure?" he asked, tilting his own head even more.

"My sister and I used to play this kind of game when we were younger. But we saw pictures in everything—tree trunks, fabric fibers, clouds, food. You have to really—look—from all angles—" She stopped and looked a bit more closely. "It's a horse, definitely. And—I think—a boat—?"

"A ship, I think," Gabriel professed on it, half jestingly. "That is kind of a strange combination, don't you think?" Aubrey nodded in complete agreement. They moved on to the next tree and studied it for a few moments.

"Well that is quite obvious!" she exclaimed. "A doll or a little girl or something like that."

"How can it be more than one thing if it's *obviously* something?" he teased her with a chuckle.

"You know what I mean." He became a little more serious.

"Yes, I know what you mean."

"Well, you try." And he did.

"Uh—it's a long shot, but I'm going to say a fish. No! A whale. It has flippers and it's blowing water from its spout." He looked at Aubrey and she nodded again.

"Yes. I think you're right." They shared a victorious smile and moved on.

"A—palette, or—something—" Gabriel attempted at the next tree. "It's too misshapen to be a clock, and those spots are probably the paint. What else it could be, I haven't the slightest idea."

"Yes, it looks like one. Sort of. And this—" She ran her finger over the other figure that was with it. "A bird, with its wings spread out. Now *that* is obvious and you have to admit that."

"Yes, I do."

They stood before the next tree, wondering if they should contain their boastfulness at having had an easy time of the pictures so far. They hoped that they would continue to have such good luck of it.

"Let me guess this one," Gabriel said. He gave it some thought and then said, "A clock gear or a cog and—another bird--?"

Aubrey's eyes lit up suddenly and she turned to him, grasping his arms with both of her hands.

"Wait! Do you know what these are? Do you realize what these symbols are for?"

"Not really."

She went back to the first one.

"Didn't your sister say she has a sanctuary or something?"

"Yes," he sighed. "Livestock or something ridiculous like that."

"The horse—that is for *her!*"

"Well what about the boat then? Is that supposed to mean that she must be with someone who would have had something to do with boats—? That is, if these symbols all represent us. I guess it could be me—we kept on getting stuck traveling with one another, and there were boats involved. But if that is the case, it would blow my theories of any of the others."

"Could it be Seamus, maybe? Or Ianto? Let's look at the other ones again."

"Yes, Seamus or whoever—did he say anything about boats?"

"No, but that doesn't mean it doesn't tie in with him somehow. You have to be making guesses to get started on stuff like this. Even if they're totally wrong. Come on—"

They revisited the second pictorial, the doll and whale not making much sense to them.

"Well, if the boat does have something to do with Seamus," Aubrey said, "Then the whale would have to be his brother—or vice versa."

"Makes sense," Gabriel agreed, impressed at her ability to code-crack. "So who is the doll?"

"I don't know. But the two birds—in both of these—that has to be Audrey and me. We would be the very most alike. So that leaves the doll to be Bonnie."

"Then that just leaves the palette to be Bonnie's twin. He had a more artistic look about him than the rest. If looks count for much."

"It must be. I would have guessed it of him as well." Another epiphany hit her then. "This must be the order that we were all paired up in!" she exclaimed. "Because we were first, and if we know that much, maybe we can figure out how to find them."

Gabriel did not want to be cynical but he was a clear *x plus y equals z* type of thinker, and this was requiring him to think a little more recklessly. Still, it was a bit on the fun side and his companion was amusing and terribly intelligent. And that the cog wheel represented himself, he could not argue that, as he saw such things daily just beneath his feet in *The Tower*. She continued on down the row of trees, the next ones not so easy to solve.

"There is a figure here, on their knees and covering their face with the another figure standing near by, and their head is bowed." At the next tree: "This one is of two standing back to back and something is at their knee level—I have no idea what that could be." She continued on. "This one—and this—" She paused, trying to determine the exact meaning of it all, but not wanting to state something incorrect. "A figure kneeling above one that is lying on the ground?"

The fun of it for Aubrey was quickly leaving. Gabriel looked them over in turn as well, wondering of them and what they were supposed to signify. Some of them did not look too promising, at least not in the way that they hoped.

"Do you think this is a *past, present, future* sort of thing?" Gabriel asked her, his voice serious and quiet, as though he feared if he said it too loudly, it would be exactly so.

"I'm not sure. But if it is, then those are *present*," and she pointed to the ones with active figures in poses. She made to move on to the next ones but she stopped before she got to them, suddenly fearful of what might be on them. Gabriel stepped along with her and stopped behind Aubrey, putting his hands on her arms.

"What's the matter?" he asked, thinking her to feel delicate and endearing to his touch.

"I'm a little—" She stopped herself. "I mean it's kind of—"

"Scary?" he offered. She glanced at him over her shoulder and nodded.

"Quite."

"It is just a game, right?" he verified. "The only rules we were given were to stay together and not lose who we're with. Otherwise—no rules."

"And to get out of the maze."

"Absolutely. And get out of the maze." Aubrey still did not budge. "We can just skip them, you know?" Gabriel said then. It did not help Aubrey to move on. She did not want to skip the next four and last trees that were awaiting her viewing and interpretation. What if they needed to know what was on them in order to solve something else? She could think of no other solution.

"You look at them," she said. "And don't tell me what is on them. Just look at them and remember and if I need to know later, you can tell me."

"I'll do even better than that," he began, taking a pencil and small notebook from his pocket. "I always have this with me. Just in case." He grinned at her and went to the trees.

Gabriel sketched out the four images, Aubrey watching his face for any give away expressions, but he held stoic until he finished. Then he returned to her, flipping his notebook closed and replacing it and the pencil back into his pocket.

"Okay. Ready to go on?" he asked.

She sighed, gave him a smile and nodded decidedly. "Yes."

Gabriel took her hand then and they passed all of the trees. It was only a short while before they found themselves at the edge of a rock quarry. It was a huge cutout in the side of a mountain of stone, granite catching the light and sparkling for a stretch below.

"Well, now," Gabriel began. "Do we scale it, or do we try to go down?"

"It looks rather steep," Aubrey observed. "I can scale the ledge, can you?"

Gabriel looked at it with great scrutiny, not caring much for either of his options, but they did not really have more than the two.

"It looks wide enough. Let's try following around."

"You're sure?" she asked him.

"Yes. It looks like there is a path just a few yards from here anyway. Then perhaps we can take that down into the quarry."

Aubrey accepted his idea, not sure if it was the best one, for it was a very long way down, but it was less steep at the pathway. They began along the ledge, finding that it was just a little wider than just wide enough, and they made slow, careful and calculated work of it. Aubrey made her way to the path easily, relieved to be stepping off onto a sturdier and broader surface. She watched Gabriel as he followed, a little more slowly than she, his eyes down on his feet as he shuffled along, kicking little rocks and pebbles down to their free-falling demise. Aubrey greatly wished that there were some way she could channel her acrobatic balancing expertise to him just then. She was just having this thought when she saw him smile impishly.

"You know, the building I work and live in is probably twice, perhaps three times as high as this quarry is deep—" he began, his gracefulness lessening as he spoke.

"Gabe—" Aubrey half warned, stopping herself, wanting him to concentrate on what he was doing.

"But being up here right now, and looking all this way down—I can't imagine it being taller—"

"Gabriel, please—" She kept one hand on her hip and the other covering her mouth.

"Because this is *very, very* high up—"

And a small pebble under his foot rolled just right, taking his balance and Gabriel gasped, losing his footing and slipping right off of the ledge. Aubrey gasped and rushed as close as she could get, lightening reflexes helping Gabriel to catch hold onto the shelf before he could fall further. He breathed hard, trying to get it back, Aubrey on her knees, because her legs had gone weak beneath her.

"Be careful—" she whispered, hoping that her heart was not pounding loudly enough to distract him, though she felt that it must be, for she could hardly breathe from it.

He took a moment to focus on what he was doing and very slowly and with a very focused strength, Gabriel pulled himself back up and he finished making his way to Aubrey. She let out her held-in breath and threw her arms around his neck, squeezing him very tightly. Quite relieved himself, he squeezed her back.

"I didn't realize that you were so—" she began, drawing away a bit. She wasn't sure what to say so she caressed his arm instead, Gabe flexing the muscle under her hand without meaning to, but certainly he was amused when she squeezed it.

"Well, I live in a skyscraper. You never know when you're going to need to do something like that."

"What do you mean? Like outside of your windows?" Aubrey asked with amusement.

"Exactly. But more likely it is from all of the years of sparring with George."

Aubrey gave him a dubious look and they began to descend by the pathway.

"Do you really fight that much?"

"The fist fights?" Aubrey gave a surprised look at his choice of words. "No, we don't do that anymore. It's really more about throwing *words* at each other. Heavy words though, usually."

"Oh."

"And sometimes heavy objects, though that is rare." Aubrey looked at him again, bemused, but she smirked.

"No you don't."

"Well, not *at* each other. Not usually. More like the general direction of." He looked at her and helped her across a small break in the path that made much too deep of a ditch to step into. "Don't tell me that you and your sister never got into a fisticuffs before."

"Not really, no," Aubrey said.

"Really? That's amazing. And impressive."

"Well, we were too busy protecting ourselves from everyone else. There was no time to fight with each other."

They reached the bottom of the pit, noticing that it had grown quite a bit warmer since their descent. They agreed that it was probably wise to get out of it as soon as possible, for they could see the heat waves shimmering across the rock and it was much akin to being in an open oven.

"It's blazing hot here," Gabriel commented, unbuttoning the mandarin collar of his white blouse. "Perhaps velvet was *not* the right choice of clothing for this place," he jested, referring to his black vest, jacket and knickerbockers.

"I hope I don't burn up to a crisp," Aubrey said. "Although I feel as though I could right about now—"

96

Gabriel's eyes went to her and the flash of sudden flame on her skirt made him gasp.

"Stop--!"

He crushed the flames between his hands, trying to put them out, the fire licking at his skin and smoldering almost as quickly as it had started. Aubrey grew frantic, knowing she should drop and try to help put it out, but she could feel the heat burning through the soles of her shoes and she feared it would make matters worse. She had no need to do such a thing, Gabriel having tamped the flames completely out, though black scorched rings remained where it had made holes in the layers of her skirt.

"We should probably run," he suggested. "And get out of here faster."

Aubrey had no objections and hand in hand, they crossed the cracked stone, the heat intensifying until they were quite sure they would crumple under the sweltering of it. They were able to reach the edge of the dig without either of them succumbing to it, and they plowed directly into a cool, waiting pool of water. They stopped there, in up to their knees and the heat coming off of them so intensely, it made steam rise hissingly from the water.

"Was that part of the clues?" she asked, catching her breath.

"No," Gabriel said, hunched over, his hands on his knees. She glanced back at the pit, her heart jumping at what they'd left behind. She nudged Gabriel's arm and he too turned to look: the flames were jumping up everywhere as though the two of them had stirred up the embers, and had they still been there, surely they would have been caught between walls of fire.

"That was too close for me," Gabe stated.

"Me too."

He took her hand and pulled her along.

"Let's go."

They left the pool after skirting its edge, their ankles still submerged. The solid ground they took to was not hot, though it was a bit marshy.

"Are you alright?" Gabriel asked Aubrey when she had grown quiet. She remained so for a few moments as they walked.

"I'm not sure." Her hand went to her forehead and she rubbed it, feeling a little pain in her temple. She was not in

97

the habit of getting headaches—in fact it was a rarity for Aubrey, and so these little twinges were certainly a red flag for her. Gabriel kept his eyes on her as they walked on, not certain that all was indeed well. Aubrey gained a few steps ahead of him, her expression one of great concentration as though she were trying to link scattered thoughts in her mind. This was in fact exactly what she was doing: she had heard a voice not too unlike her sister's echoing in her psyche and now she was trying to listen for it again. At the same instance that she did hear something—

Aubrey—

—something much darker, much larger, much more solid than a drop of rain fell from the sky and landed a few paces in front of her. Aubrey stopped walking, not moving, though her eyes quickly scanned the path in front of her, trying to locate whatever had fallen. Gabe stopped next to her, Aubrey's arm having gone up to keep him from going any further forward.

"What is it? Do you see something? Do you hear something?"

She remained still, listening, watching.

"Mm." It was a short, direct though non-definitive response.

Aubrey—

Just as the voice came again, so did another object fall from the sky to the ground, and then another and another in rapid succession. This time it made her start, but only so her eyes could try to seek it out on the muddy, grassy ground. But Gabe had seen it too, though he also remained, waiting.

But then the ground around them began to move, to jump and shift all around them. They were frozen to where they stood, unsure of what to do, and though the earth beneath them was constantly reshaping itself, they were not jostled or uprooted.

"What-is-*that*--?" Gabriel asked, seeing now that the movement was more like hopping and there were very specific shapes and motions taking place.

Where are you sis--?

Aubrey shook her head slowly, not knowing if she should pay attention to what she was seeing or what she was hearing. But the voice ended and the activity overtook her awareness and it all became very clear to her. She quickly realized that the entire ground except where their feet were planted, was completely and perpetually covered with a madness of multi-sized frogs. She gasped and grasped Gabriel's arm, not for the fear of them for what they were, but rather for the fear of their not being able to take a single step without crushing at least a dozen of them at a time. Multiple steps would result in a massacre for the amphibious beings.

"Aubrey, what are we surrounded by?" Gabriel asked her.

"Frogs—" she whispered almost desperately.

"Excuse me?" for he was not sure if he had heard her correctly.

"Frogs—" she attempted again, her voice not sounding as strongly as it should. "Frogs," she managed to get out finally. "They're everywhere—millions and millions of them—oh God, Gabriel—they're really *everywhere!*"

"I see them now," he said, his eyes having adjusted to them. "Well this is just—*ludicrous,*" he said, not knowing how else to describe it. For as far as they could see in front of and around them, the little animals were there. They seemed to hop with confusion, not knowing which direction to go, turning back when they went one way, to go back the other.

"I wonder how we're going to get out of this one--?" Gabriel thought out loud.

It was at that moment that one of the frogs jumped up onto Aubrey's skirt, the heaviness of it on the wispy fabric making her feel and see it there. Another jumped onto her, clinging to the skirt, their tiny toes like long determined fingers. Their eyes peered up at her, large and blue— humanlike almost, pleading with her for something she could not determine. She could not even pick up on their thoughts, for there were so very many of them—too many of them, and their thoughts were a terribly interwoven mess of tiny screams. Aubrey reached down on poor instinct to pluck one of them off of her, a rush of dizziness hitting her fingertips at the contact with its sticky skin. The wave surged through her hands, her arms, into her shoulders, hitting her head with a sensation akin to when she would stand too quickly from a crouched position. She held the thing up in front of her to look at it, both hands around it now, but she was losing all train of thought.

"Hey—" Gabriel began, raising his hand to touch her, but stopping before he did. Aubrey turned her head to him, still grasping the frog as though she could not let it go. It wriggled in her hands but she was oblivious to it now, her eyes suddenly draining of their color, and only the foggy whiteness remaining where her irises and pupils once were.

Gabriel gasped at seeing this, and then he noticed that the frog was becoming alabaster white and solid—it had stopped moving—while Aubrey's hands and wrists were taking on the green-blackness of the frog. The color was staining up her arms rapidly and he could see that she was hardening like marble right before his eyes.

"Aubrey--!" he shouted, hoping she could still hear him from somewhere within the shell of her body.

He saw that she was slipping away from her self as the seconds sped by, trying to think of a way to get the animal out of her death grip without touching it himself. He gave his pockets a quick search, finding his pencil and notebook. He pulled the pencil from the spiral binding, the pages flipping open to one of his crudely scribbled images:

It was of a woman standing next to a man, her hands up in a praying fold before her. There was nothing else to the drawing except a long thin line coming from the woman's chest, and the man's arm raised up above it.

"*Oh, no way*—" he breathed, feeling suddenly ill. That could only be himself and Aubrey. He knew that the images in the drawing had to be the two of them—their stance was so exact, how could they not be? And was she impaled with something? Did he have to stab her through the heart to end this? He knew that he shouldn't be standing there wasting time and asking himself questions that he knew no answers to, but he couldn't help it: he did not want to do this! Would he be losing her there if he did it? Gabriel didn't know that either, but he did know that if he did not do *something* and very quickly, then Aubrey would be lost to him anyway.

He took a quick look around but there was nothing of the sort within his reach—

Except the pencil: his Graf von Faber-Castell pencil.

He sighed heavily and closed his eyes for a brief moment, trying to prepare himself to do something so horrific he could hardly believe it was happening. Gabriel measured carefully where her heart was, reaching toward the neckline of her dress to bare her skin, careful not to touch it. He took a very deep breath and clenched his teeth to make the plunge. Just as he was drawing his arm up, the remaining frog still hanging on her skirt, swiped its sticky arm up and knocked the notebook from Gabriel's hand, and it fell onto the ground, scattering the frogs underneath it. He stole it back up, swiftly knocking the frog cleanly off of her with the notebook, the drawing then catching his tear-blurred eyes: the long line depicting the object puncturing the woman's chest was shortened—it went through her upraised hands but never reached her heart. He realized then that the mistaken line must have been a fiber or perhaps he had not seen it correctly, having been in such a panic. But now Gabriel knew what he was supposed to do and he did not waiver about it in the least, though he felt his insides quaked with too much adrenaline.

"On your life—" he whispered, instead jamming his writing utensil in between her fingers and the frog, praying that it would not snap in half as he pried the now-stone thing from her grasp. The frog's little arm broke free from its torso and her fingers, then the other.

"So it's going to be that way, is it?" Gabriel muttered, seeing that Aubrey's face was still soft, though her consciousness was far away and quite unreachable within the wall that was quickly overtaking her from the inside out. He kept on chipping away, working the frog from her, trying carefully not to damage her at all.

The frog's head came off and Aubrey suddenly gasped, taking in a deep, soundful breath, and realizing as she came around that she could not budge anything but her face.

"Gabriel?"

"Happy returns," he said, somewhat relieved.

"I can't move—" she stated, panic in her voice.

"I know. I'm working on it."

"What happened?"

"I don't know." He whittled away at the lower body, knocking the back legs off. "But when I get you free, promise me you won't touch those wretched things again."

"Sure, alright. Why can't I see?" she asked then. "Is it night again?" He afforded her the slightest glance.

"You will in just a moment. I hope," he added with a mumble.

She remained frozen in her state, hearing a scraping, almost carving sort of sound. Her slowly returning vision let her see that the look on Gabriel's face was very solemn and very concentrated. She laughed and the sound was pleasing to his ears.

"You look so serious," she stated. He half-shrugged, half-nodded, feeling every bit so, though he softened knowing that her observation meant her eyes were clearing. Aubrey was beginning to feel a vibration in her fingers and hands, the jarring of Gabriel's movements not getting past her wrists.

"Why can't I move, Gabe?" she asked softly, not wanting to disturb him at his work, but also needing to know why it felt like everything but her face was in some kind of numb oblivion.

"You're sort of—" he paused, searching for the right words. "Marbleized."

"I turned to stone?" she asked in disbelief. Again, a half-shrugging nod. He tapped her arm with his pencil and the sound was hard.

"Almost. I'm really not sure if I can explain it. Not even if I tried."

"That is different," she stated dryly.

It seemed enough for her for the moment and Aubrey said no more.

"Are they still there?" Gabe asked her of the frogs all around them, after a few moments and after having freed one of her hands from the other.

"Yes."

"A lot of them? Or not as many?"

"A lot. Like there were before."

"Well, when I get you unstuck, we are going to have to get through them and I think we are going to have to just run right over them to do that."

"That is going to be very messy," Aubrey stated.

"Yes, it is," he agreed positively. Only bits of the white remained in the crevices and folds of her palms, but it was enough to keep her motionless.

"Do you remember what happened, a few moments ago?" Gabriel inquired. "Did you just black out? Or did you go somewhere?"

Aubrey tilted her head to ponder over it. Gabriel noticed the change and his eyes lit up.

"You moved!"

"I suppose I did," she agreed, smiling. She tried to move her arm down but it still wouldn't budge.

"Hm. Still a bit more here. You must have squished the frog in your hands and these are the guts, solidified."

"That is grisly," Aubrey said humorously.

"That it is."

She went back to his question and gave it some more thought.

"You know, it was just blackness for a moment, and then there were colors and some strange swirling and sensation and kind of a chemical or biological explosion—and then everything was still and very quiet."

"Interesting. What do you suppose that was all about?"

"You know, this sounds a little crazy, but—I think that maybe it was something like the moment of conception. Only—"

"Only?" he afforded her a glance, glad to see that the discoloration of her skin was receding.

"Only—I was alone. Audrey wasn't there with me." This thought made her uncomfortably serious and painfully lost.

Gabriel stopped what he was doing and touched her clothed arm, not caring that it may not be safe to touch her yet, for lending the comfort was more important just then.

"I am certain that nothing has changed there," he assured her. Aubrey moved her hand then, touching his arm in return. The realization of her ability to move was refreshing, encouraging and enough to get her to try moving her feet. She lifted them alternately, shaking the pins and needles from them, holding onto Gabriel until they were fully restored.

"Are you ready?" he asked her then, grateful to be putting his pencil back into his pocket.

"Do we have to do this? Really?"

"Unless you think you can fly us out of here," Gabriel teased. "I could carry you but if I were to go down, we would both go down."

"Hm. I see what you mean. Okay. Let's go before I think too much about what it is that we're doing."

She brushed her hands together, the last of the white—now powder—dusting off of them, and then she took Gabriel's hand. They both winced but began to run, the crunching underfoot not nearly as terrible as the slickness that worked hard against their balance. But to fall and touch any of the frogs—dead or alive—would prove a heap of trouble for them both.

They did not stop until the population of frogs grew less and less, and eventually it vanished. Gabriel and Aubrey paused to see where they had ended up, Gabriel taking out his notebook again. He opened it to the image that had portrayed their recent events and scribbled it out with his graphite.

"Do you want to see?" he asked her, offering the book to her. She seemed afraid of it and shook her head in refusal. He gave a nod and did not push it. Instead, he looked at the others, trying to study them but getting next to nothing from them: one figure doing a sort of handstand on the other's upraised arms; a figure carrying another in their embrace; two figures facing one another in an unexplainable stance; before he shut the book again.

The glade they began to walk in was wide and open and only a scattering of trees and an occasional shrub sprang up from the grassy ground. It was beautiful and natural and seemingly untouched by human hands.

"I wonder if anyone has ever been in this maze before," Aubrey said. "Or are we the very first ever to come into it?"

"Guinea pigs, probably," he remarked, meaning the two of them and their siblings.

"You are probably right. It's kind of disturbing, and yet sort of an honor at the same time."

"Yes, to both."

Their stroll brought them to a mausoleum, the cement cube of a building the only structure around. Gabriel tried its heavy door and it opened freely.

"Should we?" he asked her.

"There doesn't appear to be anything more around— except more of the same. Let's try it."

And so they went inside, leaving the door open and lodging it ajar with a decorative urn meant for flowers or flame. It had neither in it but dust and cobwebs. Still, it served its purpose and let a stream of light into the empty tomb, illuminating a stairway that led further down into the ground. Taking hold of hands, Gabriel led the way, taking the steep descent very carefully and slowly.

"Why does it seem like we're constantly going down and down and down?" he asked with a laugh.

"Shh!" Aubrey hushed him, remembering what had happened the last time he had been talking and performing such a precarious task. "Be careful—" But she smiled as well.

The steps seemed to go for a very long while, and at one point, Gabriel mentioned that he was not looking forward to the climb back up. Aubrey admitted to herself that she wasn't either, but she did not say so, for they at last stepped off of the last stair and into a large open room. It was sparsely lit by a hidden source, and filled with widely spaced pedestals, all of them having a jar or urn or other vessel on top of it. The light came up from the top of the podiums as well, giving just a hint to what was in each container, though it was very much just a mixture of color and water and something more solid that they did not care to dwell on deciphering.

They made to cross the room, hoping not to get too terribly caught up in the curiosities, and they found themselves staring at a large, clear vase full of dark red, watery liquid. Like the others, it appeared that there was something in it, but this was almost fetal, and it was loosely swathed in a misty black swirl. They could not tell exactly, for the light under and around it was so dark and indistinct compared to the others. Aubrey felt a slight empathy to it, but Gabriel felt curiously enmitistic.

"I have such an urge to-to shove it over—" Gabriel said.

"Don't you dare!" Aubrey stepped in front of it and there was no way that Gabriel was going to remove her from his way.

"I wouldn't," he said. "But there is something about it—I can't stand it!"

"You don't even know what it is," she argued. As if to give its own opinion, the lid began to rattle against the top of the vase, and Aubrey moved away from it, taking Gabriel with her. They looked back on it to see that it stilled and it left them both wondering if they had really seen or heard it do such a thing.

"I wonder—" Gabriel began, pulling a bit from Aubrey to take a step toward the vase. She clung onto him, not wanting him to get too close for fear that he really would knock it over. "I do wonder—*Georgina*—"

And with the utterance of his sister's name, the liquid suddenly turned crystal clear, leaving no trace that there had ever been anything in it but simple, translucent water. He did go to it then and Aubrey went with him, both of them touching its smooth curved shape. It did not feel solid under his touch as it did to Aubrey, but it was more like a very thin membrane.

"I *so* know this—" he said softly. And the second he removed his fingers, the entire thing burst, covering only him with its contents. Aubrey jumped back, though completely untouched. Gabriel closed his eyes, wiping off the fluid and shaking off his hands and though he at first looked quite perturbed by it, the expression transformed and he looked more hopeful.

"What do you suppose that was all about?" Aubrey asked cautiously.

"I think George and I just made contact." This made Aubrey grin and Gabriel rolled his eyes and smirked, before taking her hand again. "Come on."

They worked through the cavern, the room of vessels ending and bringing them to a very brightly lit room with a glass ceiling. The floor was in a black and white diamond pattern and there were floor-to-ceiling rococo framed mirrors on every wall. Aubrey let go of Gabriel's hand and spun around in the otherwise empty ballroom, her face tipped up to the skylight.

"This room is incredible!" she said. "I can't believe how much sun is getting down in here—we must be about three stories below ground!"

Gabriel walked the perimeter of the room while Aubrey continued to twirl around and watch herself in the mirrors. He touched each giant pane of reflective glass, all of them taking his fingerprints but he was amazed that they did not remain—simply they were absorbed as though the mirrors had their own internal cleaning mechanism. Still, he also found that they were all solid, none of them having passages into them. With his persistent searching, he did find a door at the opposite end of the room from the one they'd come through. He opened it, amazed that it was disguised so well in the pastoral design, but not so impossibly hidden that it could never be found. Behind the door was a dark corridor but it was short from what he could tell, and at the end of it was a stairway leading upwards.

"Hey, I found a way up," he said to his companion, who now lay on the floor in the middle of the room, looking up at the glass.

"It must be gorgeous in this room during a full moon night," she mused. "I wonder if grand balls are held in here with nothing but the moonlight as light. Or maybe they bring in fireflies to make it bright. Now that would be a sight—"
She giggled at all of her silly matching rhymes.

"Aubrey—" Gabriel began, still at the door. "It's a tomb."

"I know, but still."

The sunlight began to be speckled out very slightly by white droppings onto the glass above. She squinted up at it, trying to see it better.

"Is that—*snow*?" she asked, still not sitting up. Gabriel came to where she was, looking up as well and sure enough, the sky was becoming whiter with clouds where it had before been blue and the flakes were falling more and more. But this was not to be where the peculiar change would end, for just at that moment, two figures walked above them on the glass, pushing the snow with their feet. She recognized them immediately.

"Oh my God!" Aubrey cried. "That's Bonnie! And Ianto!"

She sat up quickly, letting Gabe help her too her feet and she ran to the door.

"Come on! Let's catch them!"

He was right behind her and they made for the cold, slick stairs, climbing them as fast as they could, though the steepness of them was nearly impossible to take quickly. They slipped several times, Aubrey catching herself so she would not topple down onto Gabriel and wind them both up at the bottom and on the landing. It was a long and frustrating climb, Aubrey finding herself near tears from it, the exhaustion hitting and challenging even her heightened endurance. She wondered if it would just be faster to go back the other way, but she didn't think the climb would be much different.

"We won't make it in time!" she lamented, her chest hurting from breathing in so much dust from the steps.

"Just keep going," he encouraged. It was a frightening angle that the steps were taking, and it was starting to invert their incline. "We've got to be almost there," Gabriel said, and then with a whisper added, "*Please let us be almost there.*"

And they were nearly there, Aubrey crawling out into a room matching the one they'd found in the first mausoleum, once she'd reached the top. She was on her feet in seconds, running for the door, this one having a gray and clear stained glass window in it of a defeated looking angel. She grabbed the knob, twisting and pulling on it but it did nothing except to turn repeatedly and lost in her hand.

"Wait—" Gabriel said, having caught up with her and seeing that there was more to the door and getting through it than by conventional means.

"Hurry, Gabriel! Hurry!" Aubrey could see Ianto and Bonnie still, heading toward the crypt that they'd first gone into. But their door had a series of gears and wheels on it, needing a prompting move before it would budge and unlatch.

"Hold on, sweetheart. Give me a second—"

He studied it carefully, and then started a few of them turning, pushing hard for they were terribly rusted and reluctant to shift. There was some loud creaking and clanking and at last the door was free. Aubrey waited for it to be open only enough for her to slip through before she was out and running as fast as she could for Ianto and Bonnie, who had already entered the cube and shut the door. Her path was terribly uncalculated and though she had witnessed the two of them walking across the glass with no trouble whatsoever, it did not warrant her the same courtesy. Instead, there was a terrible splintering sound and she burst right through it, catching onto the edge of the brittle glass.

"Aubrey!" Gabriel shouted from behind her, trying to skirt around the edge so he would not fall through it as well.

"Go after them! Hurry!" she shouted.

"But—"

"Go! I'll get myself out!"

And as Gabriel ran to the door and found that it was securely and forever sealed shut, Aubrey felt the glass crumble in her hands like sugar and she grasped hand over hand, feeling the glass break off in gauged shards. She remained as calm and focused as she could, trying not to remember that there was no net below her and she did not want to now test her ability to hold in screams against broken bones. It was enough that the glass was cutting an angry red line through each of her palms, sending a heavy pouring of blood down her arms, like red leaden streamers. Gabriel gave up on the door and awaited her at the end of the skylight, thankful that she was nearly there. She did not stop for a second, or for one additional breath, the glass never ceasing to break off and the snapping sound of it was like the ticking of a clock. When she was just within reach, he grasped her by both wrists and yanked her up onto the solid ground, holding her down onto its solid surface and squeezing the breath out of her. She gave in and felt the unbearable pain in her hands and she screamed and screamed into the muffling velvet of his vest. There was no rhyme or reason to it, but Gabriel could not help himself and he thought better of trying to find an explanation for what he was next to do: he sat up above her, her screaming having subsided once she gotten them out, but her shock still racking her hard. He took her shaking wrists in his hands, pressing the bloody mess to his mouth and kissing each palm in turn. Her trembling stopped completely, immediately, as did the incessant bleeding, leaving her in a warm and protected state. When she clenched her fingers into fists to hold in the kisses, the pain was gone. Quieted and stunned, she looked at Gabriel. His eyes still held concern for a moment but when the light of curiosity in hers dropped to his blood-smeared mouth, he grinned slyly.

"Never underestimate the power of a kiss," he teased.

"Or that of utter banality," she returned with a sigh. It did not sway his grin, nor did Aubrey want it to, and he dipped his head to hers to steal a quick one from her lips.

"You are a devil," she said to him, caressing the side of his face with her quickly healing palm as she watched his eyes sparking their green fire.

"I should say the same of you, madam."

He moved and she sat up. Together, they peered over the edge and saw how far down it really was, a dreadful trail of glistening glass and splattered blood below.

"I'm surprised you have any left in you," Gabriel said, wiping off her face and then his yet again, onto his shirtsleeve. Aubrey sighed heavily and lay back onto the grass. Gabriel leaned over her.

"We'll catch up with them," he promised. "I guess it just wasn't supposed to be now."

She sat up again.

"Maybe we'll see them cross through here," Aubrey suggested, looking back down into the ballroom.

"Maybe."

"Can we wait? Just for a few minutes? It shouldn't take them very long to cross through here. They've got to be down the stairs by now."

Gabriel agreed to it, wanting a few minutes to rest after nearly seeing Aubrey plummet to who-knew-what kind of end.

But time passed and the snow continued to fall and the sky was becoming darker, and still Ianto and Bonnie did not enter into the ballroom below.

"I don't remember seeing any other doors once we got into the crypt, do you?" Gabe asked her.

"No. They would have to come out eventually—wouldn't they?"

"Has anything else around here worked out as it seemingly should have?" he queried.

"No."

Gabriel opened his notebook, showing Aubrey his sketch of a person kneeling before another who seemed to be suspended below and then he scratched it out.

"Do they get any worse than that?" she asked.

"I don't think so. But then again, I really didn't think this looked like much of anything."

"I hope they're not trapped in there," Aubrey was saying.

"For all we've just gone through, I am sure they will find ways out of their obstacles as well." Silence passed between them. "How long should we wait?"

Aubrey shook her head, disappointed when she looked down into the ballroom again and still, there was no sign of the others.

"Maybe we're just not supposed to meet here," she suggested, wondering when their adventure was going to come to a close so they could all go home and continue on with their lives. She said this to Gabriel as she stood with him and they made their careful way around the gaping hole in the ground with its thin, ice-like cover.

"Why? Aren't you having fun?" he joked, hooking his arm through hers.

"Are you?"

"Tons. I wouldn't trade this for any boring old day. Besides, I think this is the longest I've gone without running into my sister."

"But, you *did*," Aubrey pointed out as they shuffled through some sand that over-took the grass.

"Oh. Thank you for the reminder. I had *almost* forgotten."

Aubrey laughed.

"Despite what you think—you *need* her. And she needs you."

Gabriel made a disgusted face and shuddered, though he still smiled.

"You sound like our mother. She swore that some day we would need one another."

"Is this not *that* day? Or night? Or whatever?"

He held her hand as she jumped up onto a driftwood log, though it was more for the sake of touching her—he knew well that she did not need his assistance. He gave her a gentle tug and she bent down toward him, her face nearly in his.

"*No.*"

They stopped at the end of the log, Aubrey jumping off next to him. They were staring out over a red and violet desert, the sun already set and an Aurora Borealis of some sort was taking over the sky. It ran and waved in sunset colors, lighting upon the enormous desert rocks that were stacked on top of one another, small to large and monstrous boulders balanced impossibly at the tops of the stacks. They could only keep watching it, the display mesmerizing.

"It's like the end of the world—" Aubrey breathed.

"Yes. Except that it keeps going."

"Forever."

"Speaking of forever—" Gabriel began after a pause.

"Yes?"

"Will you stay there that long? Performing in the circus, I mean?"

She looked at him then, breaking her gaze from the phenomenon in front of them.

"Forever?" He looked at her then too and she laughed. "Probably not. Why? Did you want to see us perform?"

"I've already seen that," he said. But Aubrey could see the mischief flickering in the jade of his eyes. "I thought maybe sometime you could come and scale the outside of my building with me."

She grinned, immensely enjoying his flirtatiousness.

"You're impossible."

"After all we've seen and done—do you believe there is such a thing?"

"Not really."

Aubrey thought of the blond stranger who had come to take her sister away. She had not wanted her to go and she was thankful that he had not come to Audrey again after his proposal. It wasn't that she didn't want her sister to be happy—but there was no telling where she would have ended up. She felt she could better trust Gabriel—for what they had been through together already. Judging from his disdain of his sister—if it could be called that—he did not seem to have worked hard to get through the maze's challenges for the sake of saving Georgina. Perhaps he did, but Aubrey wanted to believe that he was doing it as much for herself as he was for himself. And there was less mystery to him, Aubrey reasoned, than the man who had shown up for Audrey. Gabriel made no insistent promises, as the other man had, no pledge of money and he did not try to entice her with something he knew she did not have and probably desired.

"Audrey must come and scale your building as well," she tested.

"Absolutely, she may."

She was satisfied that she felt Gabriel would hold to his word.

"Maybe all of us should get together again," he suggested. "This hasn't all been entirely bad—" He looked at her hands as he said this, seeing that they were completely healed. He could not help but to kiss her palms again, though they did not need it of him. "We could have a do-over, doing something that doesn't involve us to go off without the others." Aubrey smiled and closed the space between them, slipping her arms around him.

"What do you suppose we are to do next?" she asked. "Is this where we're supposed to wait for everyone to catch up with us, do you think?"

But Gabriel had been watching out into the distance over her head, his hand rubbing her arm lovingly. He stilled.

"No. But I think that is—" He pointed out into the desert at a flash in the midst of the sun-setting sand. Aubrey turned and looked and though she saw it as well, she shook her head slowly.

"That's a mirage. It has to be."

"I'm not so sure."

"Of course it is—look at the heat waves. There are three more flashes going on just like it. See? There, there and there—" And she pointed them out to him.

"Exactly. But those, my dear, are *doors*!" He took her hand and began down the rock, helping her down by lifting her around her waist.

"You're mad."

"Most likely. But even so—it couldn't hurt to go find out. Are you rested?"

"Yes, but even still," she was protesting. "If they *are* doors, how do we know which one is ours? They're not exactly close together, Gabe."

"All the more reason to get going, right? And I think that they're not just doors, but *the* doors."

"Definitely, you are mad." But despite what she said of him, she smiled and went with him, her hand holding tightly to his.

Chapter Fifteen
Georgina and Seamus

The very moment the door closed behind them, Georgina began to talk.

"I cannot tell you how glad I am to be rid of him! I swear he follows me everywhere I go! Well, he doesn't really, it just seems that way. Always turning up where I am, or maybe I turn up where he is. Well, I'm sure that does happen some of the times and maybe it isn't completely his fault. Still, my skin crawls when I see him and there's nothing anyone can do to help that, and it is really pathetic, isn't it?"

Seamus did not answer right away and Georgina realized that she was rambling.

"I suppose I shouldn't talk about the little creep like that, should I?"

"Well," Seamus offered, "he is your brother."

"That shouldn't really make any difference, should it? Brother or not, twin or not. We have never, and I do mean *never*, gotten along. Seems kind of funny that we've been put in this mess together. Oh! I don't mean your maze is a mess, I mean, the situation, I guess."

"It is strange, I suppose," Seamus agreed. "That you two don't get along like people stereotype that twins do. It is just that you look *exactly* like one another." Georgina groaned. "So it's a bit to get used to."

"Ugh. Don't say that. It's bad enough that it's true."

"I am sorry. But—it's eerie, you know? It's like you'd be looking in a mirror. I didn't know twins could be identical but not be the same sex."

"Yes, we are a curiosity for that, that is for sure. Say, why do you suppose everything is so black?" Georgina observed, rambling again. "Aside from the supposed time. Did you ever notice that time doesn't seem to flow for you and your brother the way it does for other people?"

"I'm not sure why it is so dark. And yes, I did notice that," he admitted, a bit relieved that the odd happening of time was not isolated to only himself and Ianto: where their guardian had seemed to gain five years of life for each one of theirs for instance—it did not end with him but everyone else around them. Their lives were lifetimes for others.

"Yes, it's like that for me and Gabe too. It always has been. I never really paid much attention to it before, but all this talk about your projects and your brother and your ages—it didn't make any kind of sense before but now I guess it kind of does. By the way, you and your brother look nothing alike. Though you've probably been told that before. Kind of strange to see twins that—*aren't*. I know that happens, but I guess it's more common than say twins like Gabriel and I."

"Yes, very true. And we've heard that quite a bit. Those other two—the brother and sister, Bonnie and Beau were they? They didn't look too similar, but there was something about them that made you know that you just couldn't doubt that they are twins."

"Right. And I'm not even sure it was something physical about them. Maybe something—spiritual?"

"Totally something you couldn't see." Seamus agreed wholeheartedly. "And speaking of such impairments: I expect that we should probably pay some attention to where we are now so we can get out of here."

"I'm with you." Georgina began to take a few steps away, her arms outstretched. Seamus touched her shoulder lightly.

"Try to stay close. We have to be sure we end up in the same place."

"Is that how it works?" she asked. "You have to agree on your surroundings?"

"Something like that. Then it will materialize."

"Oh. Thank goodness I'm not with Gabe! We'd be lost forever and ever, were that the case!" Seamus expressed quiet amusement. "I guess I got lucky, being with one of the labyrinth's designers," Georgina said gratefully.

"For what it's worth, I suppose," Seamus said.

"No, really," Georgina insisted, reaching out toward him and feeling her fingers brushing against his shirt. "This is going to be incredible—I can tell already!"

"I hope you're right."

"I've done a lot of traveling, but nothing compared to this so far. So can we imagine we are anywhere?"

"Can we influence our surroundings, you mean?" Seamus asked.

"Yes. Like if I say, 'wow, I really love that fountain over there in the garden! We should—'" Georgina stopped, her next words forgotten as she really did see a fountain in a misty garden.

"Yes, you could say something like that," Seamus agreed as he noticed the light lifting as well. Georgina reached out to him and grasped a hold onto his suspenders, pulling him closer to her. He was about to question what she was gawking at, but she pointed and he followed. He saw the garden too.

"Good-good choice," he said in a hushed voice.

"I love gardens. I love nature," Georgina said. "I love that this one has such a big flower bed," she rambled. "Oh! And it looks like it even has friendly animals roaming around—*aww, look--*!"

Seamus saw that she was looking at and running right for a flock of lambs and something struck the fear in him.

"Georgina, *wait!*" he called after her, running to catch her.

She arrived at the lambs before he did, but he was relieved that when she went for them, they moved just out of her reach. He caught up with her, out of breath, taking her hands in his and away from the wooly creatures though she laughed with eagerness to make contact with.

"They are so cute!" she exclaimed.

"Don't touch them," he warned.

"Don't touch them? Why ever not? They're just lambs."

"I know what they are, but I'm not sure *what they are*, if you get my meaning."

Georgina was not sure what to think.

"I don't. You mean, they might be—they could be some kind of—"

"I don't know. A trap, a trick, I'm not sure. Just, don't."

"Okay. All right. You would know more about it than I would. But they're so *cute--*!"

They stayed still for a moment, the lambs circling around aimlessly but as Seamus and Georgina watched them, they realized that the animals were beginning to swarm around them a lot more like sharks than the gentle creatures they were supposed to be.

"What are they doing?" she asked, feeling that she and Seamus were getting pushed closer and closer together in order to avoid being touched by the animals. They began to swirl faster and faster in their circular sea, more and more of them. They were suddenly looking more red than white, as though they'd been splattered with red paint—or worse. Both Seamus and Georgina saw this change and they came even closer to one another.

"I'm not sure—"

"Well, I know one thing," Georgina began, thinking that she was hearing some low growling coming from within the animals. "This garden might be a lot better *without* these sheep—"

And it was with that statement that everything there in their reality gave a few quakes, leaving the two of them suddenly alone again. A pause and a wondering look passed between them as they waited to see what would happen next. Things remained as they were—serene and beautiful, and waiting as well for their call.

"Does this mean we have control over what happens while we're here?" Georgina asked in wonder. "Do you know where those—things came from? Are they coming back?"

"I really don't know—about either. And I think it may not be control, so much as influence."

"What's the difference?" Seamus shrugged.

"Well, it isn't certain that if I say 'it should start pouring rain' that it will indeed start to pour rain—"

No sooner had the words left his mouth that black clouds rolled in over their heads and it did in fact unload quarter-sized drops of water onto their heads. Georgina sighed and closed her eyes for a moment, seconds only in the downpour making them soaked to the bone.

"It would be great if it was sunny again!" Georgina shouted through the noise of the pour and gesturing to the sky. Seamus nodded.

"Sunshine and no rain would be perfect!" he agreed. With their simple words, the sky cleared again and they remained, still dripping wet. He frowned. "Sorry about that."

Georgina shook off her hands.

"Well, at least we know how that works, right?"

"Yes."

"Right. So no touching animals and no suggestions on the weather," she said jestingly.

Seamus smiled and nodded in agreement.

"Right."

"Okay then. So now what do we do? We can't just stay here."

"I guess we just start walking more. Things will only really change if we do."

They wandered on, skirting the garden, though Georgina would really rather have walked through its beauty. It seemed that this way was much safer. She did not feel that she could argue with Seamus, as he knew more about the place than she did—even if that was not by a whole heck of a lot.

"So, you are in *The Sanctuary*?" Seamus asked as they continued on. Georgina smiled fondly at the mention of it.

"Yes. I have had it since it was built. No one has ever been in it but me and my rescued pets."

Seamus found this to be interesting, for he was certain that Georgina could not be very old, and yet the sanctuary had been erect for a long while. Still, the motion of time did not exactly match up for himself and his brother in accordance to the other twins and their buildings. He could not figure it out.

"What made you come up with the idea?" Georgina asked. "To have made it to look like a Trojan horse, but for what it's used for—it is such an original design. Well, I imagine that they all are, but a barn-like structure that also looks to be made as though it were a gigantic 3-D puzzle? It's ingenious and so outlandish. I really do love it, you know?"

"Ianto and I both love puzzles—we had dozens of them when we were little and our parents were still alive." He held onto that memory for a moment, feeling bad that he did not remember his parents enough to miss them much. He continued. "We used to mix all of the pieces up in one really big box and then try to piece them together and make something new out of them. Sometimes we were able to get pretty far with it—making forts and igloos and what have you with them. Funny, we have not worked one since we were children."

"And then you just came up with the idea for *The Sanctuary*? How? Why that? Did you know that that was what it would be used for?"

"We thought it would be a nice idea, and yes—we knew that it would be for that exact purpose. The materials from the extra pieces could be shredded and made into nice soft beds for the animals."

"They love that too, you know," Georgina added, smiling. "And it is amazing that for animals, they keep their beds quite clean. That is how I know they love to lay there. That was such a perfect idea: mixing the animals and a childhood favorite. It's sweet."

Seamus smiled. He was quite pleased that the person who had taken over that particular building of theirs seemed to suit it so ideally, and that her heart went into her work. But her compassion for the animals was so completely reverse of her behavior with her brother—he could not understand it.

"Why is it that you and your brother are so argumentative?" he inquired, hoping that he was not overstepping boundaries in asking. Georgina did not seem at all offended by the question and began her answer with a scoff and a smirk.

"Gabriel and I have never, and I do mean *never* gotten along."

"Why is that? Did one of you do something to the other?"

"We've both done plenty to each other. As for what started it—I have no idea. I don't think Gabe does either. All I know is that as far back as I can even remember, we have fought like there is no tomorrow—" She stopped walking and silenced as she thought over her choice of words. Seamus caught her phrasing as well.

"Perhaps you should stop fighting," he suggested. Georgina gave half of a nod, and they continued walking.

"We probably should," she agreed. "But that would feel so—*unnatural*. To him as well, I am sure."

"Who do you think started it all?" he inquired then, expecting that Georgina might lay typical blame on her brother. He was a little taken aback when she did not.

"I'm not sure which of us started it all. Maybe it was some kind of extra powerful chemical reaction when the egg split, like our own half was trying to get away from the other." She laughed. "It's funny—ever since we left our family home and went our separate ways, it is like we can't stay away from one another. We are these horrifically over-powerful magnets that keep crashing together despite one another. Isn't that crazy?"

"Well, opposites attract."

"That is the strangest thing of all: we are just alike. Though he'd never admit it out of principle, Gabe loves animals as much as I do. He would never get into such a profession because he knows *I* do it. Just as I would never revolve my life around numbers though I could out-calculate most people I know. I absolutely love where he lives. It probably doesn't seem like it would suit me but next to my sanctuary, that tower is one of the most beautiful creations I've ever seen. Though, it's like he's tainted the idea of it for me or something, and even if I didn't have *The Sanctuary*, and he wasn't there, I don't think that I could ever live in *The Tower*."

"I wonder what would happen, did you two decide to come to some sort of harmony with one another," Seamus suggested.

"Oh, we would die," she stated quite factually. "We're not meant to get along. Not even a little."

"Do you hate each other?" Seamus asked.

"Oh, *no*! Not in the least! We love one another—we just can't stand each other."

"Interesting."

"At all," she reiterated. Seamus nodded, accepting this fact.

They took another look around at their whereabouts. They were still in the garden and it seemed as though they were walking past the same flowers, the same gardens, the same fountains repeatedly.

"We really should do something about this," Seamus said. "We can't keep staying where we are."

"What do you suggest?" Georgina asked. Seamus thought on it for a moment.

"Well, in our original design, Ianto and I had tunnels that you could go through."

"How did you get into them?"

Seamus looked around, the fountain in the distance catching his attention. He pointed to it.

"There—" And he hurried toward it, Georgina in his wake, and they were in moments looking into the clear water of the pool and wellspring.

"*That*? We have to go in--?"

"By going through that? Yes."

Georgina gave no dissent, just a sigh.

"Well we're already soaked," she said in good humor, taking the first step into the water. Seamus smiled, thankful that she was such a good sport about it all, and he climbed in behind her.

"It's strange—" she began, wading into greater depth. "It doesn't look like it's that deep, but it really is."

"There should be a door somewhere at the center, from where the water is shooting out," Seamus explained. Georgina took a great breath and dunked under the surface, Seamus just behind her. There was no door in the middle, but an empty doorway, the water running impossibly in front of it and past it, but not through it. She looked at Seamus and they both shrugged, wondering of it, before Seamus went through the doorway first. Trusting that it was safe to do so, Georgina followed right behind him.

They stepped right out of the water into a room that was dim, but for the light coming in from the fountain's opening. The water ran like a shimmering, transparent door.

"Very bizarre," Georgina said, wringing out her clothing a bit, nodding at the water and how it did not rush into the room.

"Quite," Seamus agreed. They observed the room then, only one corridor leading them out of it.

"These tunnels aren't very cozy," she stated, once they were in them. "I would have thought they'd be more like the kind in stone castles, or rabbit burrows at the very least," she teased.

"Well, they're one of those—" Seamus pointed to the flickering light at the end of the hall where it started to curve. "Torch light?"

They reached it in moments and saw that the tunnel continued on and on. They maintained their journey, noting that it was a bit repetitive, as their walk through the garden had been.

"I can't say that I want to be here continuously," Georgina said. "I do hope that we are actually getting somewhere and not having a repeat of where we were."

"I understand," Seamus said. "This will have to shift again soon."

"Shift—" she restated. "Kind of like we're not actually going anywhere—we never had been going anywhere and the only change is visual?"

"Maybe so. Like the entire labyrinth is rotating so we're really only going in circles."

"Oh, don't say that," Georgina beseeched of him.

"Well, not all games are linear," Seamus pointed out. "It's possible to make a journey without actually going anywhere."

"I suppose this could be true. But then how would we know that we've finished with it? How will we know if the journey is done?"

"I am hoping that we will have found our siblings again at that point."

"It is too bad none of us really knew anything about this place—we could have chosen a meeting spot."

Seamus was amused.

"How convenient that would have been."

"Well there must be some way of getting messages to one another. There must be," Georgina insisted. "What were the blond girls saying? We can connect with each other? Or something like that?"

"Yes, I think they were talking about telepathy."

"Well, I know I can't do that with Gabriel, nor would I want to take part in that mess of a brain of his, but maybe you can with your brother. You two have more of yourselves in this place than any of the rest of us, really. Try to link up with him. Maybe you'll find that you know more of this place than you thought."

"Like subconsciously."

"Yes, exactly."

"I wouldn't know where to begin, to be honest with you."

"Well, does any of this look familiar to you? You know at least some of what this place is supposed to have in it. Can't you just think about what you're seeing and kind of push it toward his thoughts?"

"I could try to describe what we're seeing here, though there isn't much to these tunnels, is there?"

"Not a heap."

Seamus thought about the tunnels as they continued on, but his thoughts began to wander to his brother in general and not really about anything they were seeing. He imagined the other places they had had built, the opera house coming to mind. It was a shame they had yet to go to it and see a live performance gracing the stage. It was for just a moment that he felt as though it were Ianto walking with him in there—or rather, *he* was walking with Ianto. The realization of his having just made some kind of connection with Ianto broke his concentration and Seamus's thoughts brought him back to where he was with lightening fast speed, and like the slamming of a closing door. He paused, Georgina's hand on his arm. Seamus looked at her, her eyes bright and eager.

"You got him, didn't you?" she asked, and before he could answer: "You *did!*"

Seamus could not keep from smiling too.

"Sort of. Probably not as it should be, but I felt something."

"Let's try to get back above ground," Georgina suggested. "Maybe that will help. Maybe you aren't equipped with *subterranean* telepathic ability," she teased. "What was it like? Did it feel strange?"

"Not really—" It was hard to think of the right words to describe what he'd felt. All he knew was that it had made him a little tired.

"Well, try again later."

It was not long before their tunnels began to narrow and the once-cemented and stone walls and floors became of dirt and roots.

"I think we've found your rabbit burrow," Seamus teased. Georgina snickered, having to get more onto her hands and knees to get through it as the ceiling lowered.

"At least it seems to be an upward climb," she stated.

"Very true."

"I wish I had known there was going to be some getting a little dirty in this venture," she said. "I would have dressed quite a bit more appropriately."

"I think you're very appropriately dressed," Seamus jested, thinking that it must be a bit difficult getting through the burrow with her long, wine velvet skirt in her way. He did feel a bit sorry that it was probably being made for ruin. He mentioned this and she laughed.

"Don't be sorry—" she said. "I have several of them. Besides, it's just a skirt." She shared a half-laugh, half-groan. "I can only imagine what the twin girls are getting into, with those pristine white dresses of theirs—do you think they're still clean?"

"Most likely not!" Seamus said, feeling badly about that as well.

They made their eventual way back into the open air, the trees having turned with autumn colors, though the air was still comfortably warm. Both Seamus and his brother enjoyed the fall—he remembered the first time they had seen it after leaving their sea life. It was as though they'd gone from a world of white and gray and aqua blue to a world on fire. It had been so delicious to see, he was sure never to forget it. It was like this now and he wished that Ianto was there to look at it right alongside of him. For another moment, it felt as though he actually was. Georgina took notice.

"He's with you again, isn't he?" she said.

"Very nearly."

"See? You can do it too! Try to hold onto that. Maybe we'll figure out something more about this maze of yours."

"I hope so."

They headed through the leaf-dropping trees, Georgina catching one in her hand and smiling.

"Hey—" Seamus said. "You get a wish."

"Hm. I wish—" and she stopped, keeping her wish to herself. Seamus didn't ask her of it, greatly respecting the etiquette of wish making, but he sort of hoped it was close to what he would have wished, if not the same thing exactly.

Their fall orchard ended and a two-story high and thirty foot wide wall greeted them as they stepped out into the open. To the side facing them, there was nothing but stone and what appeared to be fanning fish tails. It seemed purposeless, though the entire place was certainly so far a lesson in nonsense, so it surely could not be any great surprise. They rounded it, their heads filling with all sorts of things to say about it and yet it was proving impossible for them to get a complete thought out. Simply, they wanted to laugh themselves blue.

For every foot-by-foot block, there was a fish's head sticking out, gawking at the air. Fins flapped and gills puffed and occasionally, they turned their heads this way or that.

"*What, is, that?*" Georgina asked, her laughs so caught up in her throat, she could scarcely breathe.

"Oh my God—they did it."

"Did what? Who did what?" Seamus couldn't take his eyes off of it.

"Whoever made the maze—put the fish in here."

"Are they real?"

"Oh yes," he breathed.

"*Why*? I mean, why *this*? What—*what*?"

"It was one of Ianto's ideas. He thought it would be a laugh. I can't believe it was actually put in here—"

"Are—are they okay?" Georgina was able to choke out. "I mean—they aren't in water!"

"Yes, they appear to be all right."

"They're very sad looking," she said after a moment. "And extremely illogical. I'm going to have nightmares for the rest of my life about these." Seamus could not help but to laugh alongside of her.

"Me too. At least, I'll never eat another one—too bad too. I like salmon." Seamus said. Georgina giggled, and pressed her hand to her mouth to stifle it.

"I already don't!"

"Well then, you've got nothing to worry about, where their revenge is concerned!" he teased. Georgina's sides were beginning to ache.

"Can we please leave? I can't stand this—"

He nodded and they left the fish wall, neither of them daring to look back at it. When they were a bit away from it and Seamus felt that he could talk without bursting out into fits of laughter, he spoke.

"I do think that Ianto was with us back there."

"Oh? Which one was he?" she joked. Seamus grinned.

"You know what I mean."

"Yes. I do." She maintained some sense of seriousness then, happy that he had been able to again make some kind of bridge with his brother.

They had left their crazy wall far behind and had calmed themselves a bit, speaking of their points of interest when Seamus interrupted their conversation at seeing a span of dirt turned sand turned mud.

"I wonder what this means?" he said, probably knowing that he ought to know better than to question the meaning of anything in the maze.

"Ask your brother. Aren't you two still connected?"

Seamus thought about it for a moment, but Ianto seemed much more distant to him just then.

"I'm not sure what's going on. The thoughts don't seem to be flowing like they just were."

"I wonder what *that* means," Georgina said, knowing that he was referring to those with Ianto.

"I don't know but I don't much like it."

"Maybe he's just inside of something and your thoughts can't get through. Like when you first started trying it, and it wasn't easy because you were underground—" Seamus said nothing to this and Georgina shrugged. "Well, I don't know how any of this works."

"You are probably right," he agreed then. "I'll try again in a bit."

He was wishing that he could connect with him at just that moment however, for within those few minutes, he and Georgina were now finding themselves quickly on a small sand bar that was the eye of a wide open space of mud and mud and nothing but mud. He was not sure what kind of advice Ianto might have given him in dealing with it. He supposed that whatever he chose, Ianto might have done the same anyway.

"We can't go through that, can we?" Georgina asked. Seamus did not want to start believing things to be impossible. Not now—it seemed too late for that.

"Sure we can. Why not?"

And so Seamus and Georgina took their first few steps into the mud. It squished and slid beneath their feet, their shoes ruined instantly. They were already into it and as it appeared that there was really no alternative, they went on. It was quickly that they found that the more steps that they took, the higher the mud was rising up their calves and then a few more paces brought it up to their thighs.

"This is a strange mud, isn't it?" Seamus asked, trying to keep positive about it.

"It's charming," came Georgina's pleasantly sarcastic remark. But Georgina had noticed it too—the mud had a very clay-like quality about it, it was so thick and a little on the slimy side. "I'm glad my shoes have straps on them, or I'm afraid they would be long lost—back there somewhere—" She pointed her thumb over her shoulder behind them.

"It's a little like shite—" Seamus dared, unable to keep from saying it. Georgina expressed disgust, though she still smiled. "Yes, that was a bit much. Sorry," he apologized.

"Well now at least we can look back on this and tell everyone that we were waist-deep in—"

"*Don't!*" Seamus stopped her. "Don't even suggest it."

"Whose idea was it anyway?" she inquired. "For putting a massive mud flat in here?"

"Not either of ours."

"Well, you said that the wall of air-breathing, waterless fish was Ianto's idea. And *that* was strange enough. Maybe his sense of humor is even weirder than you think."

"Maybe. But he hates mud. And he would never have chosen to wear an Armani suit here if he had any idea that a gigantic mud world awaited. So I'm positive this is not his doing."

"If this gets any deeper, we're going to be in serious trouble," Georgina pointed out, the mud up to their chests now. "I don't think I could swim in this, or even tread it."

"I hope it stays just this deep as well. Or gets shallow again."

"I wonder if we were to imagine it as something a little simpler to negotiate, if it would listen to us."

"Like what? Confetti? Quicksand?" Seamus suggested and Georgina laughed. "Though quicksand isn't really easy to negotiate."

"Confetti quicksand—now there's a thought—"

But no sooner had she said such a thing, that the mud was in fact turned to small, shape-cut paper. Georgina and Seamus gasped, both of them losing the ground beneath them.

"Oh, Seamus--!" Georgina cried, trying to reach for him, but he was too far from her by mere centimeters. "I'm sorry--!"

They were both fighting to stay on top of the particles and shreds, the sharp and ragged corners and edges biting into them everywhere and leaving hundreds of tiny bleeding wounds on their skin.

"Try to get on top of it!" Seamus said, though he was struggling too as the paper and plastic and foil slipped around beneath his weight. Georgina was running out of breath and as she saw Seamus turning onto his back and successfully staying afloat, she fought to do the same. It was more struggling but at last, she was able to get there too. Both of them were exhausted, but they had somehow managed to get close enough to lock fingers with one another.

"What do we do now?" she asked.

"I don't know. Let's just stay here for a moment and think."

Georgina began to lift her hand to look at the stinging cuts, but Seamus stopped her.

"Don't move, Georgina! Please—do not move. It will take us off balance."

She froze, her hand back down gently. After having rested a moment while watching the sky—which was full of constant green leaves billowing by just as if they had been clouds, Seamus spoke.

"I'm going to be picking stars and hearts and shamrocks out of places I never even knew I had, for months," he stated. Georgina erupted with laughter. Despite knowing better against it, he added—"You probably will be too—"

Georgina went into hysterics, her hand in Seamus's coming up in an effort to stabilize herself, though poorly. Seamus squeezed her fingers in an attempt to still her, the wave of paper pieces beneath them still poking and nicking them like little flimsy razors.

"Ouch!" Georgina cried, trying to stifle her giggles. Tears burned her skin as they ran down her temples, hitting every cut on the way.

"Hey—" Seamus began, noticing the color of her blood. "It's a perfect red. It is perfect, cranberry red."

She was able to quiet herself finally.

"I love cranberries," she confessed. "What if we were in a cranberry bog? At least those are only a few feet deep."

"I would definitely prefer a cranberry bog to this," Seamus agreed.

"They are beautiful to look at—like a red sea—a *cranberry* red sea, even—"

They were silent for a moment as they closed their eyes, the beating of their hearts creating a gentle rocking under and around them. The sharpness of their bottomless bed was softening and liquefying.

"Seamus—I think the confetti is getting lumpy—"

Seamus opened his eyes to see exactly why, picking one of the millions of red berries from the water and pitching it across Georgina's stomach. She did not start at the bouncing fruit or the plopping-plunking sound it made when it hit the water again, but she smiled and sighed.

"This is nice. I could stay here forever—"

She took one up herself, the two of them still afloat and she brought it to her matching lips. She took a bite of it, the skin popping, the inside spongy and crisp and sending a bittersweet trickle of juice into her mouth.

Just as Seamus had noticed that she'd done this, it was as though something had hooked Georgina around her waist and it yanked her hard beneath the cranberries—and she vanished.

Seamus gasped, flipping over onto his stomach, his feet slipping on the bottom and plunging him under. His knees hit the ground and he stuck his head out of the water with a most surprised gasp. Georgina was gone!

Seamus began trying to shove the berries aside so he could see into the water, but they replaced each other and the faster he moved them away, the faster more came to fill in their place.

"Georgina!" he shouted, moving around just where she had been, trying hard not to stray too far from where they'd just been floating, every inch of it for stretches all around looking exactly the same.

Seamus held his breath and dunked under, scanning and looking for her—any sign at all—but he saw nothing but red-tinted water in every direction. He wished he could call for her under the water, but be couldn't. Seamus resurfaced, ready to burst into tears: Georgina was no longer there. He slammed his fists down against the surface, the angry gesture producing nothing but a splashing and bruising against his hands. But then as it settled, he began to feel ripples and waves around his legs as though something was trying to wrap around them. He returned beneath the cranberries to look again. Still he could not see her, but something was there with him: a wispy, black, smoky and swirling in the red. It reached for him and he jerked back, afraid of what it could be. It recoiled as well but did not leave, some shapeless part of it reaching for him again but not closely enough. There was something familiar about it to Seamus—he wondered for a moment if it was Ianto trying to communicate with him—*could it be*? He moved a bit closer to it, careful not to let it touch him. But it was fascinating and he did not want to go up for air, for fear that it would not be there when he came back. And it was so very familiar: he began to think then of his foster father and their days at sea, scouting out the fascinating Arctic life, and the water around him began to grow very cold and the red turned blue. Still, the black smoky figure remained, floating like a ghost, trying to take shape. It kept trying to connect with him, becoming denser but never quite enough. It made Seamus sorrowful, for though it was clearly something that had life within it and his eyes perceived that it was close enough to touch, he felt in his heart and mind that he was light years away from it. He soon forgot that he needed to breathe, noticing only that as the burning of his tears came from his eyes, the water growing colder around him stole them away and the apparition's movements were slowing as though it too was freezing. Soon it would stop altogether and he felt that this would be the end of him—and Ianto.

His eyes were feeling heavy and the water's lull made him want nothing but to stay wrapped in it forever. Seamus saw the blackness getting closer and closer to him, sudden green lights flashing at him—two of them, like emerald beacons in an ebony fog. He could have no way of knowing how he'd managed it, but he made his hand raise up and he stretched toward the lights, his eyes closing as his fingertips brushed over smooth skin. He felt the cheek under his touch rise from a smile, and he smiled back.

But then his chest was feeling very tight, a crushing, viselike squeeze keeping any air from getting in. He tried to struggle from it, but he could not escape it. And then the world around him felt as though it moved very fast and there was nothing he could hold onto—but this did not matter— something was holding Seamus. There were some very hard blows coming at his chest and Seamus wondered if his heart was imploding, but the coldness around him was quickly warming and air exchanged places with the water in his lungs. He gasped and choked and sputtered, his hands reaching blindly and grasping velvet-clothed arms.

He opened his eyes, blinking hard, to look right up into Georgina's hovering face. Her eyes smiled at him and water dripped from her tresses onto his face.

"Weren't you ever told that *you're* supposed to *drink* water, not *breathe* it?"

He sat up and Georgina moved back a little, Seamus still holding onto her arm with one hand, his other wiping his face and his mouth.

"What happened to you?" he asked. "Where did you go?"

"I have no idea," Georgina said, but she seemed a bit shaken.

"Are you alright?" Seamus asked. Now that her concern for him was settled, it was as though clouds had covered over the sun in her face and she looked a little afraid.

"I think so," she whispered, though she did not look it and Seamus could see she was uncertain. He wrapped his arms around her, hugging her tightly, for whatever she had seen it had given her quite a fright.

Seamus noticed over Georgina's shoulder that they were back on land, and other than the fact that the trees seemed to grow upside down, it looked a little more normal than before. He kissed her forehead and stood, pulling her to her feet. She noticed the trees too but made no comment of them, some kind of mournfulness still hanging on her. It was not until they came to an open area between two forests some time later, that she said anything.

The grass beneath their feet was short, almost unlike anything they'd ever recalled seeing before. It was nubbed on the end of the blades, shone sort of misty in the light, and felt odd to walk on.

"Ornamental grass?" she suggested. "It kind of looks like gunpowder tea. Before it's dried, of course."

Seamus winced.

"Do be careful in saying that!" he teased. Georgina laughed softly.

"Unless you have some rogue, lit matches, I think we'll be alright. Besides, it isn't *that* kind of gunpowder."

"Yes, well, why take chances around here, right?"

They wandered around, looking at it, seeing a large and rectangular area of it sparkling in the sunlight. They went to its edge to get a closer look.

"Well now what do you make of that?" she asked, crouching down to look at it. Upon closer inspection, they noticed that it was the same grass but it was full of clear crystal shards. Georgina picked one up gingerly, careful not to hold too tightly so it would not cut her.

"There is so much of it—" Seamus referred to the crystals.

"And it isn't even part of the plants—look—" She gave some of the blades a little shake near their roots and then brought her hand up slowly, the back of it salted with the sparkling bits.

"Glass?" Seamus wondered.

"I'd hate to go through this barefoot," Georgina said, both of them agreeing on that. She thought of Aubrey's twin then, having noticed that the girl had not had any shoes on at the beginning of the labyrinth. She hoped that this was not posing any problems for her course through it.

"Same here."

Georgina stood up again, putting her hands on her hips.

"I wonder what this area is supposed to be?" she questioned. "It's not a garden. Not really. Cemetery?"

"Without tombstones? Maybe."

Seamus was wandering around the perimeter of the glassy area, looking down at it and unable to take his eyes from it. Georgina did the same, from the opposite side.

"I don't know what it is about this place—this spot, exactly—there is just something so odd about it."

"Interesting, you choose *this* exact spot to call *odd*," Georgina jested.

"True."

Seamus took a step onto the glass, the sound of the crunching underfoot sounding a bit like tiny crystal chimes.

"Hm."

Georgina shrugged and Seamus took another step onto it. Still more tinkling. He grinned and jumped up and down, knocking a lot of the crystals off of the grass.

"What *are you doing*?" she asked him.

"Not sure. But it's kind of fun—"

And he went directly through the ground just then, disappearing in a flash from Georgina. She ran around the perimeter to where he had made a hole in the ground, finding that he hung below the surface, clinging to the roots of the grass. She dropped down to her hands and knees, ignoring the little bits of glass that stabbed the heels of her hands, and she tried to hold onto his wrists.

"Seamus—"

And though he was now hanging presumably upside down, with nothing below him but clear, blue sky, Seamus could not sense any reason for concern. Everything was upside down now—or perhaps it was only he. He felt the blood rushing to his head and his hair felt to stand on end.

"Well now, this is strange indeed," he said, looking around.

"Can, can you come back up?" she asked him, thinking there to be nothing below him.

"I think the question is—" and he paused to bring his knees to the new ground, flipping himself upright, and then looking now down into the hole at her. "—Can *you* come *through*?"

"You are kidding, right?" she asked and hoped. But he had let go of the grassroots and seemed to have righted himself.

"No. Come through—"

"It's safe?"

"Do I appear unsafe to you?"

She sighed and stood up again.

"Alright then—"

Taking a deep inhale and then letting it out again, Georgina jumped up and came down hard, breaking through the ground and zipping past him. His hand shot out and grasped her before she could fall into the sky, and he brought her back to the ground, gravity righting her back to her feet. She caught her breath, holding onto Seamus to be sure she would not rise up again, seeing that he was smiling at her.

"Wasn't that fun?" she asked, half sarcastically.

"Quite!"

She took a look around, seeing that they were in a rectangle of grass matching the glassy one from the other side, and bordering it and stretching out in all directions were indigo, knee-high irises, puffed and frilly and fragrant.

"I wonder where we are now?" she said. "Are we still in the same maze?"

"We must be," Seamus said. "I'm not sure where else we would have gone."

"This is true."

"Onward?"

"Onward."

They pushed through the floral field, the yellow pollen dusting them as they went through the blooms and the sweet smell of them making them feel refreshed and hopeful.

"Life just won't be the same after this," Georgina said, pointlessly brushing the pollen off and making it worse on the mess of her velvet. To this, Seamus beamed. She noticed and drew her brows at him, though she still smiled too.

"Then it has proven itself."

"What has? The maze?"

"Exactly. That is part of what it was supposed to have done—"

"Oh. Well congratulations to you then!" she praised. "Without you and your brother, this certainly would not have come to be—even if someone else did take it over."

"I am glad that everyone in here seems to still be doing alright—at least we know Ianto and your brother are. Or else we would not be here either."

This made Georgina's arms prickle and her heart stirred. Certainly, she hoped everyone else was safe and well.

Chapter Sixteen
Ianto and Bonnie

Bonnie did not want to open her eyes after the door closed. Ianto wasn't so sure he did either, but he knew that they had to do something. He was a little startled by the sound of her voice.

"What do we do now?"

"We have to figure out where we are."

"I think I want to be back home," Bonnie said softly.

"So do I," Ianto agreed.

They remained in the darkness.

"Are you scared?" he asked her.

"Will it make much of a difference for us if I say yes?" She could tell that he smiled.

"Probably not."

"Are you?" she asked him then. His answer did not come instantly, as he debated on whether or not to own up to his thoughts. He did not have to. "You are," Bonnie said for him.

"May be a little."

"I won't tell if you won't," she promised quietly, a little seriousness restored in her voice. He held onto her just a bit more securely.

"Thank you, love."

They gave themselves a few more moments there before Ianto knew they must continue on, for nothing would change if they did not, and he took a deep breath and then spoke.

"Shall we then?" She nodded at his side. "Do you want to see the Concertina trees with their crimson blossoms?" he suggested to her. He was not sure that there would be such a thing, but if they were to play this game, he wanted it to at least have something pleasant for them to look at.

"Yes," she whispered. He dropped his arm from her but kept a firm hold on her hand and they began taking steps out of the darkness and into a fog that was quickly clearing.

"It must be spring here," Ianto was saying as they stepped through the dew-wet grass. "And early morning."

Bonnie could scarcely believe what she was seeing, the promised beautiful trees suddenly coming up all around them. They were the most beautiful trees she had ever seen and the flowering kinds were her favorite.

"Are these real?" she asked him.

"They certainly seem to be, don't they?" he said, wondering of it himself as he dared to touch the blossom of one. It felt real enough. He scanned the way the trees were arranged, seeing a little bit of a pattern in the rows and after a moment, he was able to decipher that they were making up his and Bonnie's path.

"I think we can go this way—" he was saying, pointing toward the break in the rows. She followed along with him, a few of the plucked flowers in her hand. She held them to her nose to smell them, detecting a warm, comforting amber scent to the little bouquet before she put it in her pocket and caught up with Ianto.

"How do you know this is the right way?" she asked, having no argument against his strategy, whatever it might be.

"I don't. But I suppose as long as we are still moving on to something new and don't hit any dead ends, we are going in the right direction."

It sounded as good as any explanation to Bonnie.

"What do you do when you aren't designing these, unbelievably odd and fantastic structures?" she asked him, hoping that their conversation would stay light and not remind her of how incredibly terrifying it was to be there in that bizarre world, and with a stranger nonetheless.

"Not much, really," Ianto said. "Seamus and I have made our work so much of our lives that it has not left a lot of time for anything else. It's been such a part of us for as far back as we can remember—as though it is what we were born to do."

"And you have always—until now, of course—been in on it all together?"

"Always. It seems to bring about more solid structures that way."

"It is like that for Beau and me with our art as well. Did you ever consider coming up with your own ideas? Without one another having a part in it?"

"Never."

Bonnie thought for a moment on how she and Beau had collaborated projects before: she would write a story and he would illustrate it, or he would create a painting and she would put a past, present and future to it.

"They really are beautiful, you know," she praised. "Your designs. I have only ever seen *The Monastery* and the theater, though I'll bet your others are breathtaking. We had it moved, you know? *The Opera House*, so it is closer to *The Monastery* now."

"Really? That seems impossible," Ianto said in surprise, knowing how very large the building must have turned out, not to mention everything—every detail that must have been put into it. And to his knowledge, they had originally been built very far—an entire ocean and more—apart.

"More impossible than being inside of a magical labyrinth with three other sets of twins? All who are wandering amok and watching the day turn to night and night to day with their mere movements? And more so than giant red blossomed trees that seem to spring up in the blink of an eye, when it should take them the better part of a century? More impossible than *that*?"

"I suppose not," he agreed with a grin. "How did you have *The Opera House* moved?" he questioned then. "If not impossible, then that must have been an incredible feat."

"I don't know, really. I told Beau once that I missed it, but I would not leave him to go back to it—I could not even risk going there if he had been with me, I was so terrified that I would get stuck there and never be able to return. So he had the move done for me—for our birthday a few years back. It was all rebuilt only about a mile from where we live, without my ever knowing it until it was completed. That way I am still close enough that if I feel I need to run home, it would not be impossible—even on foot."

"How did the reconstruction turn out? It must have taken a long time."

"I have honestly never found a single detail of it out of place—and I have spent many years and many hours in there. If there was a mistake—I would know it."

"That is impressive," Ianto said, pleased that she loved it so much to know it so well. "What an amazing birthday gift."

"Well, that is my Beau." Bonnie blushed and smiled at the thought of her brother and his generosity and sweetness.

She could feel Ianto hesitating to speak but after a moment, he did.

"You and your brother have a rather—*interesting* closeness," Ianto dared to say. Bonnie smiled impishly at him, detecting what he was hinting at.

"Beau would be more inclined to fancy *you* than—" She didn't finish but Ianto caught on.

"Oh. *Oh*." He smiled as well at realizing what she'd meant. "Your affections for one another are quite deceiving then."

"Yes, I suppose they are. Our *closeness* as you put it, is a little bit too *interesting* to many people. Which is why we aren't seen together outside of our home much."

"I can see how that might be awkward." Ianto was quiet as they walked and Bonnie wondered if he too like so many others thought it to be objectionable behavior for siblings. His next words surprised her: "Your bond must be of great magnitude. How anyone could ever try to sever it is unthinkable. That is really sacred."

Bonnie nodded her head, thankful that Ianto understood. She felt an overwhelming aching for her brother all of a sudden, and though she hated to be parted from him as they were, she was quite uneasy that the sensation had waved over her so intensely. Ianto noticed her slowed steps and turned to look her way again.

"Are you alright?" he asked, studying her changed expression. She found it difficult to catch her breath for a moment and to grasp her words enough to speak them.

"Yes." She shook her head and forced a smile, the feeling subsiding a bit. She stepped into Ianto's gait and slipped her hand back into his, the squeeze of his fingers around hers making the troubled feeling dissipate more.

"What about your family?" Ianto began. "Are they still alive? Your parents?" Bonnie shook her head.

"Our mother, we were told, was in a car accident while she was pregnant with us. She didn't survive. They delivered us from her cadaver. And then we were separated from each other."

Ianto grimaced.

"That's—horrendous."

"Yes. We have no idea of anything about our father. At least what each of us was told of our mother matched up. It's a morbid foundation to the facts, but at least it was solid."

"So she never even got to hold you two."

Bonnie shook her head.

"Never. In fact—I don't think we were, either of us, *ever* held, even once in our lives other than to be fed or transported, until the day we re-met."

"Not by anyone?"

"Not by anyone."

"How sad for you," Ianto lamented of it, but Bonnie smiled.

"Yes, but you must imagine the absolute bliss of it after waiting fourteen and a half years, when Beau and I were reunited."

Ianto smiled back, imagining it easily.

"It was worth it," he deduced.

"Very. So what about you? Are yours--?" but she stopped herself, seeing the change in his smile. She could tell it had been tragic. He noticed that his change had worried her and he put his arm around her shoulders, forcing a smile.

"We were pretty young when they passed." It was more the thought of his foster father that caused his heart to ache.

"I'm sorry." He could only nod, accepting her sympathies.

"You know, you do not look anything like your photos on your books," he said instead.

"My books?"

"Yes, your books. The ones you wrote."

"You've read them?" she asked, not having taken him for someone who might be interested in their overly romantic strangities. He nodded. "How did you hear about them?" she asked then, his knowledge of her at all seeming a little suspicious.

"You meet people, you learn things when you travel like Seamus and I do," he said innocently enough. "It is impossible not to discover great things in our travels. I also like that your brother did the artwork for your covers. Your works compliment each other."

"Are you sure it wasn't you who sent the invitations to this place?" she interrogated gently.

"Positively, it was not us," he insisted, looking at her. "And believe me, I would not have dreamed of putting you in such an uncertain environment. Nor anyone else. I hope you believe that of me, Bonnie."

"I suppose I must. Why would you and your brother be here, otherwise? If you think it *that* mysterious or questionable."

"Thank you." His fingers tightened around hers, his eyes falling on her again. There was nothing but the utmost sincerity in them and Bonnie could not find fault in him for her and Beau being brought there. Despite the forward instructions, they still could have declined.

"I suppose we could have just not shown," she said, speaking her mind.

"I am glad you did—" His words slipped out before he could stop them, but he was not sorry to have said them. "For many reasons," he finished.

Their surroundings were beginning to look quite familiar then, and when they crested the hill, they found that they were now looking down at Bonnie's beloved opera house. Ianto saw it and his eyes grew wide.

"Is that what I think it is?"

"Yes."

Bonnie saw a light akin to fascination come into Ianto's eyes as he continued looking down at it.

"You've never been inside it before," she said to him. He could only give a slow shake of his head. "Well--? Do you want to see it?"

He looked at his companion and grinned.

"Do I!"

With their hands still linked, they descended the hill and went to the great, carved doors. Bonnie pushed one open with all of her weight and pulled him inside with her. They took a short dark corridor that ramped up from underneath the stage and along side of the orchestra pit, trekking slowly up the cranberry red-carpeted aisle. The room was lit up with the enormous candle-filled chandeliers and the entire place was glowing red and gold. The rows of seats seemed infinite, the balconies were over their heads like golden sun chariots, carved and gilded, curtained and waiting.

"I could just stand here and stare at it all for hours—days!" Ianto breathed.

"You should see it from the top," Bonnie said, giving a little tug on his hand. He looked at her, too excited to budge.

"Did they put them in? The hidden balconies?" he managed to get out.

"Come on—" Bonnie insisted with a smile. She was pleasantly surprised that someone else was as pleased about the secret lookouts as she was, though she had kept them all to herself once she had found them, not wanting the magic of them to be shared with just anyone—certainly not the unappreciative nuns! She could not keep them from Ianto.

He followed her eagerly, taking stairway after stairway and finally they were in front of a trompe l'oeil depicting a castle wall and windows that looked out over the land. It was forever night through them and the tempting, hidden door lay between the faux stone ledges. Bonnie paused and looked at Ianto, who knew exactly how to open the door though to the unknowing eye, there was none. He did not hesitate but went through it, pulling her up the remaining stairs with him, the case narrow and enclosed. They reached the top and he went into one of the boxes, pulling the drawn curtains wide to expose the entire theater below. His breath caught as he looked down on it, his hands on the railing of the balcony to steady him, for he was so very high up.

"This is absolutely fantastic! It is more incredible than I ever dreamed!"

He gazed down on it for a few moments more before he realized that Bonnie was still standing at the entry. He turned to her, his smile softened.

"Come in?" he asked.

"Your brother had no part in designing these rooms—but *you* did, didn't you?" she asked curiously.

"Yes."

"No one has ever found them but me. What were they for?" To this, Ianto bit his lip to keep his smile from beaming and Bonnie could nearly see him blush in the shadows. He held his hand out to her, beckoning her to enter the room. When she was at his side, he wrapped his arm around her, and his smile became playful, impish.

"They were for secret lovers to escape to," he said finally. "Did you ever bring anyone to one of these rooms with you?" he dared to ask. Bonnie lowered her head before he could see her shy smile.

"Only you, just now. Not even Beau has seen them."

Ianto dipped his head just enough to see her face, pulling closer to her and tipping her chin up. She smiled more, their lips very close and she felt the corner of his mouth touch hers. Her eyes closed and he bit her lip gently, making her gasp. He kissed her then, deeply, sweetly. The passion of it grew in them, between them and they could not draw away from one another. For the sake of catching his breath and to keep his heart from beating itself to death, Ianto ended the kisses, but kept Bonnie in his embrace, conferring them still upon her head.

"Can't we just stay here until someone finds us?" Bonnie asked, listening to Ianto's throbbing heart, her ear pressed against his chest.

"It doesn't work like that, I'm afraid. All of this—" He gestured to the theater. "—is just part of us, what connection you and I are making together."

"But it's exactly the same as the one I know!" she insisted, pulling back from him but not giving up his touch.

"It isn't, love. Look—" He went to the loveseat then and tore up the velvet from one arm of it, and the frame underneath crumbled like sawdust. "See? It looks as solid as we are, but it isn't."

"You're making that happen--?" she said, jamming her hands into her espresso brown sweater's pockets and rolling a few of the blossoms between her fingers. Her head was spinning.

"I swear to you, Bonnie, I'm not. It is just what this place is here. We can't stay here—we still have to get through the labyrinth."

"If it isn't real—the theater, what am I going to go back to when we get out of here? Is that place not real either?"

"It is. *This* one isn't."

"Are *you*? Am *I*? Are you just the ghost I always imagined being in here with?" She was having a hard time keeping her thoughts straight and it did not seem right that she was standing in a place she had been in many times before and was being told that she wasn't actually standing there. Ianto felt the shift in her and he knew that it was becoming too unsettling, and for the little he did know of her, she was not quite herself now. They were in one of the traps that he had feared. He thought it best that they leave the theater before it really took hold of her.

"Time to go?" Ianto suggested. Bonnie nodded, letting him lead her back down the stairs to the mezzanine floor, to the wide staircases and then onto the main floor. They chose to take the front entrance to get out, quickly heading down a long hall of tall and narrow mirrors.

"Maybe it will be easier to think when we are outside again," Ianto was saying, sorry that a serious tone had set in, for he had truly been enjoying his closeness with her. But Bonnie wasn't even hearing him as they hurried along: she was watching their reflections as they were rushing by, and she had to shake her head to be sure she was seeing right. She stopped suddenly and pulled away from Ianto, running to one of the mirrors and pressing desperate hands to the pristine glass. The eyes she looked into and the palms that were reflecting against Bonnie's were not her own. Her eyes filled with tears as Ianto stepped up behind her to try to see what she was seeing.

"What is it?" he asked, very concerned for what he could not detect and now had her so captivated.

"It's Beau! *He's on the other side of the glass!*"

Bonnie could certainly see her brother there, relief expressed in his face at seeing her as well. She said nothing for a moment, Bonnie seeming to have come under a wave of calm and Ianto's concern turned to trepidation.

"What is he doing?" he asked her.

"He's getting something to break it with—" And truly she did see Beau searching around for something with which to strike the mirror.

"No! Don't let him!" Ianto cried. "He'll kill us! Bonnie, stop him!"

"How do you know? You don't know that!" she cried back frantically, never looking away from Beau.

"I *do* know that!" Ianto wanted to touch her, to pull her away but he was suddenly fearful of intercepting Bonnie's connection with Beau. "Please, stop him!" he pleaded instead. "You *must*! Or we'll die here and *so will he*—"

Ianto's words hit her to the core and she pounded on the glass with her fists to get Beau's attention. He came close to the mirror again, a heavy iron ornament in his hand. Bonnie shook her head at her twin desperately, not knowing that she sobbed as she motioned frantically for him not to break the looking glass.

"Tell him to keep going," Ianto instructed painfully, knowing Beau could only see his sister and it destroyed her to have to lose sight of him into uncertainty again—as it no doubt was doing to Beau of Bonnie. She did as Ianto bade her to, watching as Beau finally did leave before dropping her face into her hands. And when she looked again, he had disappeared from view.

Ianto knew Beau was gone when Bonnie sank down to the floor, giving way to her tears.

"Was Audrey with him still?" he asked, crouching down with her. She shook her head numbly.

"Couldn't, see her—" she managed to get out.

"I couldn't see your brother either, though you could. Maybe she was still there--?" But he did not sound sure of this. Bonnie's cries had grown weak and she could only let the tears continue to fall in tiny salty rivers down over her cheeks. Ianto sat with her, encircling her with his arms and holding her there in the safety of them.

"I am sorry to have made you do that, Bonnie," he whispered to her. "I am so sorry—"

And though she was there in his embrace, she suddenly seemed very distant to him somehow. He lifted one of her hands in his and raised it up to look at it, Bonnie giving no resistance to the motion nor did her hand seem to have any strength in it to hold up against his.

"You will be reunited again, do not doubt that," he was saying softly to her. "Out of here, away from this riddle we are stuck in." He could feel that her separation from her twin went much deeper than it did for the others, even for himself from Seamus. She seemed so lost at their forced parting. He wondered how they had managed their earlier years, Bonnie and Beau, having to do without one another. Ianto turned Bonnie's hand so her palm faced him and his blood ran like icy water when he noticed that he could see his own hand through hers. He sat up suddenly, lifting her face up to him. Her head dropped against the hand that cradled it, and her eyes were heavy. He touched her cheek, the skin becoming translucent. Ianto lifted one of her lids and saw that the blue-green of her iris had whitened over. Checking the other one revealed the same.

"Bonnie!" he exclaimed in desperation, taking both of her shoulders in his hands. She seemed to fade right before his eyes and he was seized in alarm: if she disappeared completely, he knew he would be trapped there.

"Be *here* with me, Bonnie," Ianto said to her firmly. "I know you want to be with your brother, wherever he has gone to, but if you don't be *here*, you're not going to *be* any longer. *Please*, Bonnie—" he pleaded. "Do you hear me?"

It occurred to him then how very grim things were about to turn and he wondered if he was going to indeed become part of the labyrinth and everything that it was not. He brought her back into his arms and leaned against the glass again, whispering against the top of her head through tears of his own.

"We have to focus on where we are, Bonnie. I need you to help me to do that. And we need to get out of here before we can even think of looking for Beau." He swallowed hard. "Come back to me—" She gave no response and he stroked her hair soothingly, not yet giving up. "*Please, love, I need you to do that for me,*" he whispered, while gently rocking her.

Very long moments passed and the long hallway was beginning to narrow. As the untrackable minutes ticked by, Ianto watched as the lights at the far ends of the corridor begin to go out one at a time, leaving nothing but darkness behind. He did not want to resign to their fate of going out like one of the candles, and they were getting fewer and fewer and snuffing out faster and faster. He pulled his feet up into the last bit of flickering light as though the pitch would devour them alive. It was seemingly close to becoming so.

"*Bonnie!*"

Her restored breath sounded painfully and she grasped her arm in her hand. Ianto did not notice. He knew only that she had returned and it took all of his restraint not to crush her to him in his arms.

"I will try," she murmured, her hand reaching up to clench a fistful of his shirt. She looked up at him and Ianto smiled at her, relived that she was regaining her solidity. He sighed and kissed her endearingly.

"We need to get out of here." She nodded, touching his face. His eyes closed briefly as he absorbed the caress and opened again at her voice.

"Where should we go?" she asked. He helped her to her feet and keeping her at his side, they began to walk through the hall.

"Let's try for that door again."

They found their exit, the candles having relit but the flames dull and lifeless along the way. When they stepped outside, it was very cold and the sky was gray. It was tempting to stay within the theater, but they knew that it could not be so. Together, they walked across the frosty grass and it crunched under their feet like glass, Bonnie shivering and her teeth chattering though she tried hard to keep them from doing so. Ianto stopped and took off his jacket and began helping her into it. He saw the trickle of blood on her arm soaking through her sweater and took hold of it to inspect the mysterious wound.

"How did this happen?" he asked, thinking it to look like a bite from a human's mouth.

"I don't know. Didn't you see anything?"

"Not a thing." He wrapped it with his cloth handkerchief. Their eyes met for a moment, Bonnie fully returned to him, and he helped her to finish getting the jacket on.

"We *really* need to get out of here, Bonnie," he insisted. If she had not been afraid before, by his tone, she was now.

Their chosen direction took them to the edge of the sea, and it looked as fierce as the heavy clouds over their heads. It took but a moment to realize that the tide was coming in from all sides of them and they were stranded on a very small area of quickly shrinking sand. Bonnie stepped back as far from the foamy edges as she could, and ran her hand through her hair.

"Ianto—this is crazy!" In only seconds, the depth of the water grew far deeper beneath the surface and it was not stopping. They were soon backing into one another with nowhere else to go. "What are we supposed to do now?" He only shook his head and went with the most logical of choices:

"It looks like we're about to start swimming."

Bonnie did not at all care for swimming, so when Ianto mentioned their needing to do so, she felt things could not become too much worse. They did not jump into the rising tide, simply they stayed where they were and let the water come to them. It did not take long and before Bonnie could try to hold her head above the water, it became very strong and quickly pulled them both down into it like quicksand. Ianto had taken a very deep breath and when he saw that Bonnie had not, he grabbed a hold of her and pulled her to him, giving her a bit of air. They were continuing to sink, against all efforts they made to try swimming upwards, and they were becoming too quickly exhausted. It was maddening, for neither of them wanted to just give up and let the water drown them there! Still, they could not fight against the invisible undertow and so further down and down and down they went. It was very dark in the water and they kept a tight hold onto each other's hands, their lungs burning at the need for more oxygen and the rapid change in pressure. Bonnie kept her eyes on Ianto, certain that she was going to implode if something did not change very quickly. Ianto looked as though he was trying to sort out a solution but he could think of nothing but giving in and letting the force take them as far as it was going to. They were both very near blackening out, when their feet suddenly hit a bottom of some sort. They peered down at their new ground, finding that they stood on a grate. All water around them was draining through it so swiftly, it pulled them hard enough to make them sit down. When they were no longer surrounded by water and instead were just drenched with it, they remained sitting, catching their breath. No sooner had they done so, did the grate unhinge beneath them and they fell for a distance more, a hard landing resulting onto a pile of shale. It was hard for them to get their balance, the slick, black pieces of rock sliding every which way beneath their weight. At last Bonnie got to her feet and she helped Ianto to get onto his. They had to catch their breath again from the fall, their bodies having taken a jolt from the rough landing. Ianto did not look pleased at their newest turn. Bonnie could only try to shake it off. She noticed as they stood there that her pocket full of red blossoms had turned itself inside out and now the blooms were scattered all over the black slate. The contrast was stunning and she could not pull her eyes away from them.

"We *are* going to get out of here, Ianto," she stated. "I know we will and Beau and the others will too."

He looked at her in slight amazement, her mood having seemed to turn completely around from her hopelessness. She went on with nearly fatal optimism—he wondered for a moment if she might be delirious.

"You will get back to your projects and it will all be such an amazing story for us all to tell when we go back home—" was her promise.

Bonnie could not resist the flowers and she began to quickly gather them up again. Ianto watched her, wondering why they were so very important to her all of a sudden. Her movements began to slow and there were so many of the flowers left—he hadn't realized that she had taken such a lot of them. Strangely, she dropped down onto the shale, forgetting it seemed, what she was doing. Her head bowed as she brought the flowers to her nose and smelled them. In an instant, she began to cry, and just as she had in the theater, she was growing distant and faint—only the flowers in her hands remained their vivid, vibrant color. Ianto rushed to her, knocking them from her hands and shaking out the ones that stuck to her skin, avoiding touching them as much as he could. Her hands remained cupped and open, tiny little red marks pocking them up from the floral venom.

"Come, Bonnie, love. Let's move on," he said softly to her, his arm around her shoulders as he stood her back up and guided her away. In moments, she had returned to herself, not knowing that she had had such an episode.

They followed the underground tunnels for a long distance, light coming in from unknown sources and only just enough to help them to see where they were going. They noticed the constant sound of running water, though thankfully light continued to follow them as they went on and the water remained only to trickle down walls and dampen the ground. They did not say much along the way and at one point, Ianto checked Bonnie's palms to be sure that the red marks from the poisonous flowers had gone away. Whoever would have put such a thing in a maze meant for entertainment? He could not help being angered all over again that their idea had been stolen and created—*destroyed* in the creation of it, for it was turning out to be something that they would not have made it: dangerous. He continued on, frowning deeply.

"You look very troubled, Ianto," Bonnie observed quietly, holding onto the back of his arm. He glanced at her and attempted a smile, though he felt more annoyed that they were still in the damp tunnels.

"It would just be nice to be above ground again," he said, not speaking other thoughts in his mind just then.

"We will be, very soon," she said. Though really she had no idea—how could she, never having been there before? Ianto looked at her again, thankful that her sudden hopefulness had come through. "The way out can't be too far from us now," she stated, positively. "Probably just around the bend. Isn't the "way out" always just around the bend?"

Ianto smiled then for real.

"Usually around some bend or another, yes," he agreed.

And their bend came into view.

"You see?" she exclaimed excitedly. "Let's go!"

She ran to it, Ianto increasing his strides to be just behind her. He found her at the end of the bend—stopped at a large, locked iron door. She smirked.

"Sorry."

Ianto sighed and touched the very solid, heavy door. It had no lock and no hinges—not even a doorknob.

"How are we supposed to even open this?" Bonnie wondered aloud. "This is the strangest door." She touched it then too and found that it was cold. "Do you think that we took a wrong turn?" she asked him. They both glanced down the long corridor from the bend, all lights from where they'd come now blackened. "Do you think this is a dead end?" she dared to ask then.

"It couldn't be," he said. "Because it doesn't appear that we can go back now." They returned to the door.

"We're going through that then?"

"It would appear that we are going to have to. But how--? I'm not certain yet."

Ianto looked over the structure of the door, felt along its edges, its bolts and bracings. His frown twisted as he thought about it a moment more. Bonnie put her hand on it again as well, feeling very small next to it, for the door was easily double her height. She sighed and looked at Ianto when he leaned against it and looked at her.

"Well?" she queried. He nodded and then shook his head, Bonnie leaning on the door with him.

"I haven't the slightest idea on how to open this door," he confessed honestly.

"Oh," Bonnie said with disappointment edging her tone. She turned her back against it, looking wistful, though she was trying very hard not to think, for that only seemed to make things worse.

"What do you think we should do?" he asked her, hoping that she would have some kind of suggestion—*any* kind of suggestion, just so they could try something.

"I suppose there is that old proverb—*if you want to open a door you have to think like a door.*"

"I've never heard of that," he teased and she turned back to him.

"Well, maybe not put in that exact way." He smiled.

"Yes, I know just what you mean." He looked at the door again, feeling along its edges. "Well then, what is the purpose of a door? To keep things or people out—or in—"

149

"Or to make a way to something or somewhere else," Bonnie suggested. He grinned at her again and then faced the door with intent.

"I like your way of putting it better." Ianto put his hands on the door, his palms flat. "So, let's go through the door—"

And his hands went right through it as though it were not there at all and he practically fell with nothing to support him at the unexpected yielding of it. Bonnie saw him as the door was swallowing him up and grasped onto the back of his shirt, closing her eyes in the instant it was happening, hoping it would be enough to pull her through with him.

With her unintentional push, Ianto landed on the ground, Bonnie falling right on top of him, both of them a little stunned at having the wind knocked out of them. He looked at her, holding her arm gently and making sure that she was all right. She checked him over as well and they smiled at each other and their having conquered their obstacle. And then they looked to where the door had been: all that remained was a wall with a clear cascade of water coming down it. It rushed to the floor, collecting into a gutter, and there was unmistakable daylight on the other side of it.

Bonnie touched Ianto's chest, lightly grasping his shirt, feeling that it was barely damp from before and then feeling her hair and the deep red calico of her dress—both were also nearly dry. They rose slowly, seeing that they had entered into a sealed room, but for the waterfall where their door had just been.

"I guess we are to go back through," Ianto said.

"Did your labyrinth plans have all of this stuff in it?" Bonnie asked him.

"I suppose some of it," he admitted. "But it was a while ago that it was thought up—and after being in here for a while, I can't tell anymore what was ours and what was someone else's."

"Well, you conceived the original idea," she pointed out. "So *all* of it is yours."

He only smiled at her and took her hand, before he stuck it with his under the water. It splashed back on them and she squealed, wiping off of her face.

"Looks like we're going to get very wet this time," he warned.

"Let's get it over with then."

They both took a deep breath this time and as they passed through it, the water was very heavy and thankfully not icy cold. Rather, it was tepid and they did not cross through it without it making them both feel rather sleepy. When Bonnie and Ianto came through and out of it, they found themselves stepping up out of a blue tiled pool, water spraying down over top of them like a segregated rainstorm. They climbed out and sat on its edge, wringing out what they could of their clothing.

"This looks very familiar," Ianto said of the fountain.

"It does? How so?" Bonnie wondered. "I'm sure we haven't been here yet."

"No," Ianto concurred. "Maybe *we* haven't. But I think that maybe Seamus has."

This made Bonnie stand, excitement striking her at the idea of it.

"Really? Here? Your brother—here?"

"Yes, maybe."

"How would you know it for sure?"

Ianto smiled at her, happy that she was smiling.

"I don't really. Just that it feels like he has."

Bonnie stood up and walked around the fountain, coming back to Ianto quickly.

"Do you think it was long ago? Should we look for clues? Would he have left something behind?"

"I think it may have been recently, though I don't know if he would have left any clues. If I remember correctly, no clues can be left by those who are in the maze."

"Like us," Bonnie suggested, her hope falling slightly.

"Yes, love. Like us."

"Why not?"

"Well, Bonnie," he began, caressing her cheek. "Because that would be cheating."

"We have next to nothing to go on as it is—"

"I know."

Just as the disappointment was setting in on Bonnie's face, her attention was suddenly drawn away from him and to something that she saw in the grass a short distance away. It looked like a worn down stone foundation of a wall or a building's frame and she went to it quickly. Ianto stood, watching her from the fountain's edge.

"Bonnie—"

151

But she fell to her knees, pushing the grass aside to free the wall, a shiny black object nestled in among the green blades. She picked it up.

"This is very, *very—unbelievable—*" she mumbled, picking it up.

"What is? What did you find?" he went to her, and Bonnie held the object up to him: it was a lone chess piece. "Peculiar."

"Yes," she said softly, knowing it well as she took another look at it, but she was unable to place it. She handed it up to Ianto and he took it, looked it over and returned it to her, smiling warmly. She gave it one more turning under her gaze, wishing hard that she could identify it, before she put it in the pocket of her sweater and took his hand to let him help her up. He embraced her, knowing where her thoughts were just then, though she did not seem quite so forlorn as she had the last time such thoughts had drawn her mind. He could feel more hope restored in her and it was slightly contagious. He could now understand why her bond was so strong with her brother: it was enticing and embracing, comforting and safe. She drew away from him, his hand holding onto hers until it no longer could unless he too moved, and she started walking around in wide circles on the grass as he remained where he was.

"What if we are supposed to just stay where we are and let the others catch up with us?" she wondered. "What if the more we move, the more we just all pass by each other, making it impossible to ever meet up?"

"I suppose that is a possibility," he agreed. "But then, what if all of us thought that and all of us stayed where we were—and we never came to the same spot."

"Hm." She crinkled her nose at him and went to where he had returned to sit at the fountain's edge. "That would be bad, wouldn't it?"

Bonnie frowned as Ianto nodded.

"The odds are great that we will all come across one another eventually," he promised, holding his hand out to her.

"It could be a long time," she said, taking it.

"Mm." He agreed.

"It could be a very long time." He smiled, seeing that her mood was ever more playful. "A *very*, tremendously long time—"

"It can't be so long, love," he insisted, kissing the top of her hand. "We *do* have to conclude the game, and for that, sooner is probably better than later."

"What if we are actually enjoying the game?" she advocated, grasping the hand that held hers and he pulled her closer to him at her mock resistance.

"Getting out of the maze does not indicate the end of all," he suggested.

"Doesn't it?" she pressed, his arm slipping around her back, Bonnie's hand still caught in his. His head shook slowly and drew her very close to him.

"No, it doesn't."

"When we leave here," Bonnie started. "Maybe you would some day like to see your opera house for real."

"It would be a first." Ianto warmed at her invitation. "Perhaps we should make a visit to all of them?"

"Perhaps you should make your first visit to the secret balcony of your choice," she suggested, her eyes having dropped to his lips.

"I will make it a priority," he promised.

She took Ianto's face in her hands then, kissing him and setting fire to the passion already building inside of him for her. He held her face when their kiss ended, his seriousness catching her off guard.

"Ianto—"

"Let it be known that I have enjoyed every moment of this with you," he said. "Even the parts of it that have not been so kind."

"As have I," Bonnie confessed, wishing his smile would come back, for the pain in his eyes—or perhaps it was fear—making her uneasy.

"You are a beautiful little doll," he said. "I wish I could put you in my pocket and keep you always next to my heart."

"And why can't you?" she asked.

"You would have to leave your Beau now and then for that."

"He would understand," Bonnie assured him. Ianto's brows rose.

"You would leave your home—and him, to come with me?"

"It is only when our having to part is against our will, that we fear it."

His smile returned fully and he embraced her.

"Then when we return home, we will look into making some plans."

She pulled away enough to look at him.

"Do you think that you and your brother will have anymore masterpieces made?" she wondered of him.

"Yes. That is for certain."

"What does your own home look like?" she inquired then, letting him pull her to sit on his knee, still in his arms.

"It is a cottage, really. Small—enough for the both of us."

"Why only a cottage? You have all of these other fantastic places made, and you yourselves do not live in one?"

"We are not home often enough to have such a house."

"Well then, your cottage: what does it look like?"

"It is a gentle, heaven blue—like the summer sky when the cirrus clouds are wispy and faint. The gingerbread trim is white. The front door is made of frost-patterned glass and the handle is of sterling and shaped like a Nouveau sprite—"

He stopped when he saw Bonnie shaking her head in disbelief.

"How now—you don't believe me, love?"

She shook her head again, and pointed over his shoulder. He turned to see at what she was gesturing to, scarcely believing his own eyes, for just behind them in a quickly falling fog was his and Seamus's house. They stood and he took her hand, going closer to it, but approaching it slowly for fear that it might disappear. Still a bit away from it, but close enough to tell that it was indeed the same, they stopped and Bonnie looked up at him, her eyes lit up by her smile.

"Are you ready to go home, Ianto?"

Chapter Seventeen
Beau and Audrey

When Beau and Audrey stepped through the door and it closed them into the blackness, they did not move. Neither of them spoke for a moment and as they were a few feet apart, Beau began to wonder if he was alone.

"Are you still there?" he asked.

"I think so," came Audrey's quiet voice.

"What kind of place do you think this is?" Beau asked her. In the dark, Audrey shook her head, not knowing whether or not to make a guess.

"Hopefully a typical kind of maze, with walls and turns and paths—"

As though dawn was rising, they were able to see then, the walls in front of them made of stone and the walls around them of brick or hedging, path breaks appearing sporadically.

"Are you very good at these?" Beau asked her while reaching out to touch one of the walls.

"I'm not sure."

"Me either. Somehow it's always a little easier on paper," he jested. She gave a little laugh.

"Yes, well, that is because you can see the entire thing all at once. But this—"

"This is very strange." They were in definite agreement about that.

They took their path slowly, the walls going on and on, breaking here and there, turning every so often. Occasionally they would see something different: a marble statue of a Greek God or Goddess, or a sculpture of metal or a glass window that only let them peer into another corridor that appeared to look exactly like the current one they were in. It seemed to be endless, nothing much changing and though they tried to keep their conversation going, they often fell silent, lost in their own thoughts and wondering when they would come to the end of the maze.

"It is strange—" Beau began as they rounded another bend. "I have not seen or heard a single bird since we've been in this thing. We *are* outside, aren't we?"

"I thought we were—" Audrey began, but before she could finish her thought, a cardinal landed at the top of the wall and chirped at them. They both smiled, though it was odd too. The creature did not stay long and fluttered away after a quick looking in on them.

"I wonder—" Beau thought out loud. He stopped walking, still looking up toward the top of the wall. "How tall are you?" he asked his companion.

"I don't know," she answered. "Probably five foot something. Why?"

"Come here—"

She went to his side and he made a foothold for her to step up into.

"See if you can get a better view—"

Audrey stepped up onto his hands with her small bare feet and he hoisted her up as high as he could, her bare feet stepping up then onto his shoulders.

"Anything?" he asked, steadying her.

"Yes—" She grasped the top of the wall and pulled herself up onto it, the rough stone abrasing her skin. She gained her balance and stood on it, scouting out the area.

"Well?" Beau questioned, craning his neck to see her.

"Walls—" she began. "Walls and walls and walls, as far out as I can see."

"What about back in the direction we came from?"

"I'm not sure" she started doubtfully. "I can't tell exactly what direction we even came from."

"That doesn't sound good."

"We have made so many turns—it's very hard to tell where we started from. Though it certainly doesn't seem like we've been going on as long as it seems it would have taken us to get here—" She gazed out at the tops of the interweaving walls some more, trying to untangle them and find her way back from where they'd come. "We must have been moving along pretty fast," she said finally. "I just can't tell where it begins." She looked down on Beau. "I'm sorry."

"It's alright," he told her. "Maybe you should walk up there for a while? You could probably navigate us better from up there."

"I'll try." He smiled at her and followed her lead.

"You do that very well," he observed after a few moments had passed.

"Oh?" she said. "What is that?"

"Walking up there. Like you are an acrobat or something."

"Oh, I am," Audrey said, nonchalantly. "My sister and I are. In a circus."

"Wow," Beau exclaimed. "I've never met anyone from a circus. That must be a fascinating job."

"It is quite exhilarating," she agreed.

"And the height doesn't bother you, obviously."

"Not at all. Aubrey doesn't mind it either."

"I can't stand heights," Beau confessed. "At least not without something solid to hang onto or lean against. Then it's okay."

Audrey laughed.

"Then this will really freak you out—"

Beau looked up at her and she did a round off handspring back flip on top of the wall. His heart jumped at the terrifying thought of her falling off. And worse—falling off onto the *other side* of the wall. Especially as he did not know yet how to get to the other side. He gasped and covered his eyes with his hands, half-teasingly. But Audrey had executed her gymnastics perfectly and she landed on her feet, just as she should. She laughed at Beau's scare and she walked along at a more careful and calculated pace for his sake.

"And what do you do?" Audrey asked of him then, waiting for him to catch up with her as she made another turn above him.

"I paint, create music and the like."

"You make your living off of it?"

"Yes, of course. Bonnie as well—she writes."

"Oh. I will have to look for your work sometime. And hers. I love to read. If only I could read and swing from a trapeze at the same time—I'd get so much more done in a day."

"You could have your sister read it to you," Beau suggested.

"I could have her read it to herself and I would still hear it."

"You are that good at communicating with each other telepathically?"

"Yes. We are that good. School, for the short time that we went, was rather awful. The teachers and the other students—they did not make it too easy for us. After a while, it was actually impossible to try to learn." Audrey did not

157

elaborate, the memories of her mother and the rest of the population she and her sister had mortified by the gift making her feel disdainful. Beau detected this at once and made to change the conversation slightly, on her behalf.

"Well, it's certainly an unusual and exceptional talent."

"You don't find it to be weird?" she asked him.

"Not at all. In fact, that kind of thing is probably responsible for how my and Bonnie's lives were able to cross again. Neither Bonnie nor I find those things to be *weird* as you put it. Nor metaphysics or any of the mystical arts. She has seen more than her share of ghosts or spirits, or whatever you want to call them."

"Have you?"

"Seen ghosts? I've seen enough not to question that there are things out there that are just not for understanding."

"Fair enough," Audrey accepted.

"How are things looking up there?" Beau inquired then.

Audrey stopped and looked about, shaking her head a little and twisting her mouth into a frown.

"It's looking about the same. I can't help but wonder if we are going in a circle."

"It isn't going in a circle that would be bad," Beau said. "It's if we are going in a circle and not making any progress."

"Well, in that case," Audrey began with a sigh and then looking down at him. "It does not look like we are making any progress."

Beau sighed as well, not wanting to hear such an update on their affairs in there.

"I wonder if we could mark something—" he speculated aloud. He looked around for something to make a marker with, but could only find a few stones on the ground, and small ones at that. They would have to do. "Here, catch this—" He tossed them up to Audrey and she caught them, before setting them at her feet. Then they continued on.

"At least we have decent weather here," she observed. "I don't mind a cloudy day but did you ever notice that birds don't seem to fly much in the rain?"

"If at all," Beau concurred.

"It is the same for us. We can't do our aerial acts if there is a storm."

"Interesting. Is it for fear of lightening?" he teased.

"Not so much as it is a sleeping hazard."

"Meaning?"

"Meaning that it makes us so sleepy—we don't pay attention to what we're doing. We drop like flies."

"Very interesting."

A few turns later, things began to become more and more uncannily familiar. Still, the few stones Audrey had placed on the wall were not reappearing. She stopped, her expression one of frustration.

"Something doesn't seem quite right," she stated. "I don't know what it is, but—something—"

"Well maybe we should leave something that is easier to see," Beau recommended. He searched his pockets and found a black knight from a chess set in his jacket pocket. He couldn't just then remember where he'd gotten it from, and it was quite possible that Bonnie had put it there without his knowing. She was good for doing that—slipping treasures into places where he was sure to come across them. "What about this?" He threw it up to her and she set it on the wall. "Can you see that better?"

"Let me see. Stay where you are—"

Audrey went a short distance down the wall and turned back, just in time to see the wall swallow the knight up!

"Oh! No, no!" She grasped her head in her hands.

"What?" Beau asked, wishing he could see at the wall's top. "What happened?"

Audrey was hurrying back to where she'd placed the chess piece, running her hands over the wall's surface and the few feet before and after it.

"It's gone—it's *gone*! The wall just—*took it*!"

"Took it? Like it ate it?" he half teased.

"*Exactly* like that!"

"Oh, that is brilliant," Beau mused with mock enthusiasm but he could see that she was quite serious.

"I—I never would have believed it if I had not just seen it—*sink!*"

"Are you sure it didn't fall off? Or maybe the wind knocked it over--?"

"I'm sure. There's no wind up here. Oh!" she wailed. "I can't *believe* this!"

"Now what?"

Audrey groaned and looked around, trying to think of an alternative. Nothing came to mind.

"We have to think of something else," she supposed. "Or we're never going to get out of here."

"Let me know what you come up with," Beau said, following along the wall at a slower pace, his hand running along the stones. Some of them were as rough as pumice, he noticed and some of them were smooth like marble. He also discerned that they were not all the same temperature to the touch. He wondered if that meant that some of them were movable. He tested this theory, coming to very little conclusion. He sighed and wondered if Bonnie was having better luck. It was good for them to be apart now and then, he considered, but he did wonder if they would have been having an easier time of it had they been allowed to stay together.

"I think this truly is to be an exercise on how to work with our twin, without having them here to help us," Audrey deduced, speaking practically every thought Beau had just been thinking on the matter. "Seamus made a good call when he mentioned that."

"I imagine that you are quite right on that," he harmonized. "Do you think that may be working for anyone else?" he questioned.

"I am not certain. I could try to find Aubrey—Should I?"

"Please."

Audrey sat down on the wall, not able to concentrate enough as she stood. She closed her eyes and thought about her sister, wondered where she was and even asked it of her. There came no answer, not even the littlest of sensations of her twin's thoughts coming in return.

"Hm. It is so strange—"

"What is that?"

"It is like there are walls around her and nothing is getting through to her."

"Like talking to a wall?" Beau played.

"Yes, I guess it is just like that."

"So then talk *to the wall*," Beau instructed.

Amazingly peculiar as this sounded to her, Audrey did not doubt that her companion might actually have something in that. She straddled the wall and lay on her belly, her ear pressed against the stone. She listened for a few moments and then put her forehead against it, thinking her thoughts to her sister:

Aubrey—

Still there was nothing. She tried again:

Aub—where are you? This time, she turned her head and pressed her ear down to the stone, and there was a sound reverberating back to her. She gasped and sat up in surprise, not having expected the wall to answer her. She quickly put her head back down on it to listen more.

The sound was slight, but the voice was Aubrey's. She waited just a while more but the answer never came more clearly.

"It has to be working," Audrey said, before she stood up. "I will try again in a few minutes. We may as well press on until then."

Beau was amazed. Though he knew he shouldn't be—for wasn't their being there in that place mind boggling enough as it was? Nothing really should surprise him. Still, knowing that two people could use their minds to speak to one another—it was a little much to swallow at once. He shook his head to himself as he continued along below Audrey's lead. What about himself and Bonnie? Was their reunion as it had happened ages ago not awesome in itself? Perhaps even more so than telepathy—finding someone who was not looking for you and with nothing to go on but your heart? The thought of her just then made his cheeks flush and burn and a swirling of butterflies swooped in his stomach. Knowing that Bonnie was probably feeling those sensations, Beau had complete faith in Audrey's talented gift with her sister.

"I am at war with myself," Beau began, "between wanting to be back home with Bonnie, and being thankful that we are here having this experience."

"Same here. Though what is it exactly, that we're supposed to be getting out of this, I wonder? Is there some kind of lesson to learn, or are we just supposed to experience this for whatever it is—a game that two brothers came up with and someone took over from them? Is it a huge plot of revenge?"

"To my knowledge, Bonnie and I don't have any enemies. Although, that may not be up to our discretion."

"Aubrey and I don't have them either. We don't get the time to make enemies. At least, like you and your sister—not intentionally."

"Maybe it could just be something that we will come away from, never knowing truly what it was all about."

"Well, I hope we know something by the end of it," Audrey said. "Aubrey's thoughts are really jumbled to me, but we must be at a greater distance from one another than we've ever been before."

"I wish that Bonnie and I could do that—in words anyway. I do feel what emotions she is feeling, when she wants me to, and I always know just before she is going to come to me in the night—"

Beau stopped mid-sentence, one of the windows in the walls seemingly longer than the other windows before it had been.

"What is it?" Audrey asked him then, looking down at Beau and seeing that his gait had slowed down. He did not answer her but paused in front of the window, seeing movement that was not his and when it moved quickly along the wall through the clear pane, he hurried to follow it.

"Beau?" she asked, agilely moving along the top to keep up with him. The expression on his face changed to one of hope and fear all at once and he began to run, his eyes never leaving the wall as he passed it by, except to glance in front of him to be sure he did not run into another one.

"What is it? Beau?" Audrey shouted, trying to keep her eyes on him and keep her balance as she ran as well.

"Bonnie's on the other side of the wall!" he exclaimed, still following his sister. But suddenly he stopped and Audrey could see him going to the window and pressing his hands to the glass, his gaze peering into it with desperate intensity. Audrey looked down the other side of the same wall and her knees felt weak as she discovered that there was nothing on the other side but more of the same path that they were on. Certainly there was no one else there. She knelt down on top of the wall, trying to look down into the window, but it was blackened from her angle.

"Bonnie—" he said softly, knowing that she probably couldn't hear him.

"Beau, there's no one there--!" Audrey insisted.

"She *is* there!" he insisted back, turning away and looking for something heavy to break the glass with. "She can see me too—" He found another odd sculpture of wrot iron and he pulled a scepter from a strangely shaped jester of sorts. He hurried back to the window, ignoring Audrey's pleas for him to help her off of the wall. He could scarcely hear her, his eyes locked with Bonnie's as she stood not even an inch from him. Her face was distressed, and the tears were rolling down her cheeks in streams. Beau could not stand the sight—the pain of having her so close and so distressed, and not being able to get to her was maddening. He raised the scepter, ready to strike it and free her, but the complete and sheer terror in her eyes stopped him. Bonnie began to shake her head at him, one hand covering her lowered eyes as she began to wave her hand at him for him to leave. She did not stop, looking up at him again and begging him silently to go away.

"Beau—" Audrey landed with a hard thump on the ground beside him, but still he would not budge. His heart ached and he did not want to continue on—not without his sister. He barely felt the tugging on his arm, and when she resorted to yanking hard on him, Beau dropped the scepter and went with Audrey. He took a few steps with her and she let go, looking back after a few seconds to be sure he followed.

"What happened?" she asked him. He followed her like he was lost, somnambulant.

"She was in there—my Bonnie was in there—" he was saying. "She didn't want me to break the glass—she didn't want me to get her out of there—" He looked at Audrey, the tears pressing into his eyes. She waited for him to catch up with her. "It was so horrible!" he grieved. "She was so *insistent*, but something was wrong—I didn't see Ianto in there with her." He stopped, his steps still slow next to hers and Audrey put her hand on his shoulder.

"I am so sorry, Beau," she whispered.

"I have never so clearly seen her heart break like I just did," Beau confessed, feeling the ache and guilt as well. "I promised her—I promised—"

"You didn't break your promise," Audrey assured him. "You just can't get to her yet, that is all." After a moment she added: "You have a very close connection with her." She smiled and Beau afforded a smile back, though he was feeling anything but happy at that moment.

"I wish there was something I could do. And I would—you know? I would do anything for her." Beau stopped speaking and they continued on.

"Well, that is a great love you have for her—" Audrey's words caught in her throat as she looked at Beau and saw that he was beginning to grow fainter. She rubbed her eyes hard.

"Yes, we certainly do have that—" Beau was concurring. He ran his hand through his hair and his movement blurred like spilled ink mixing with water.

Audrey grasped his arm and he stopped moving and faced her.

"What is it?"

"What is happening to you?" Audrey asked suddenly. Beau looked at his arms and hands, seeing that he was growing quickly transparent.

"I don't know! I don't feel quite right—"

"It's your sister—she's pulling you into it!" Audrey quickly explained as she realized what was happening.

"She's what?"

"Pulling you in! To the maze. You're connection is *really* strong with her—you have to tell her to let go of you!" She took a hold of his other arm, nearly feeling her own fingers coming together where his flesh should have been. "Beau—you're disappearing!"

"What should I do?"

Audrey was shaking her head, trying to think of something but her mind was suddenly blocked and she could think of nothing but five words:

"Tell her you love her, tell her you love her—" over and over again and nothing else coming to her mind. "*Tell her that you love her—*"

"I do love her," Beau whispered, feeling sleepy and vague. The young woman continued to repeat her words, and it was hypnotic, powerful. He wished that Bonnie were right there with him just then so he could tell her those words. Could it be that he had never said them to her before? He couldn't remember just then. Did she not know it anyway?

Audrey was speaking to him but he could no longer hear her, Bonnie feeling closer and closer but he could not see her and he could not touch her. He felt as though his legs were collapsing but he could not tell if they did or not. He reached out and felt that he made contact with something, but he could not grasp it. But it was deceiving and what he felt of her in his heart was being pulled farther and farther away. It was as though the closer he got, the farther away she moved. Something was wrong but he did not know what. He could only know that she had never been more removed from him than she was becoming and it was reducing him to nothing.

But then there was something—a sharp and deep pain that he could not locate, but it was bringing him back very quickly and the sting became like fire. He opened his eyes with a start and found that he was on the ground, Audrey kneeling next to him with his arm in her grasp and a little blotting of blood on her lips. Seeing that he was conscious, she let go of him as though he were a hot barb.

"I'm sorry!" she apologized, her hand against her chest, the other reaching toward him but not touching him. "I didn't know what else to do—"

Beau looked at his assaulted arm and saw the deep marks her teeth had made in his skin.

"What just happened?" he asked, sitting up.

"You were—almost *gone*. You dropped and I couldn't wake you—I'm sorry. I-I bit you," she blurted out.

Beau sat for a few more moments to clear his head, Audrey sitting eagerly and embarrassed at his side. He looked at the perfect dents and partially broken skin and then looked at her.

"Wow," he said. He took a glance around at their surroundings, which had changed to dusk again, and they were no longer trapped within the walls.

"This is so strange," he stated. Audrey nodded in agreement.

"Welcome back," she said. Beau laughed.

"Thanks."

She helped him to stand and they looked around, trying to choose a course of direction.

"You know, somehow it almost seemed easier when we were within the walls instead of in this wide-open space," Beau said. Audrey agreed with him fully.

"I wonder how the others are doing?" she said.

"Do you think they're doing as well as we are?" his question was only hinting at sarcasm. "Your sister—would you at least know if she was alright."

"Oh yes. I am not sure why I cannot grasp her words clearly, but I can feel everything she does." Beau looked at his arm where Audrey had bitten him.

"Do you think Bonnie felt *this*?" Audrey shrugged, a sorry and guilty look on her face.

"I hope she didn't."

Beau wiped the blood off with his shirt, seeing that Audrey had not broken the skin and only the marks remained. He reached out to Audrey and tipped her chin toward him, looking at her lip—she had bitten down onto herself, right through him: it was her own blood.

"Are *you* alright?" he asked. She nodded vehemently.

"It throbs a little but I really didn't know that I did it, I guess." She rubbed her finger over her bottom lip, giving it a little healing massage. "We have an incredibly high pain threshold," she threw in there. "My sister and I."

"How is that?"

Audrey shrugged.

"It was part of our training in the circus. Probably to help us channel the pain were we ever to fall and break bones or something. You know—so we wouldn't traumatize the audience with a bunch of screaming and carrying on. We never did though. At least, not yet."

"How did you train for something like that?" Beau asked with great curiosity.

"It involved a lot of breathing. And being apart for periods of time—"

Beau's thoughts returned to the window that Bonnie had been in and he turned suddenly, running back into the maze to look for it.

"Wait! Beau—" Audrey called after him, running to catch up.

But Beau was stopped abruptly at a dead end—the window was no longer there and neither was their previous path. He felt along the stones, knowing that they were immovable and then looked at Audrey.

"I-I think the wall sealed itself off—" She nodded in agreement.

"I don't think we're supposed to go back, ever," she said. "I mean, in life—you can't go backward either, just forward."

"But you can return to somewhere you've been. Isn't that the same thing?"

"Going backward and returning are not the same," she attempted to say. "Because you are never the same person when you return somewhere, so you can't go to where you were. You're not even the same person every time you wake up in the morning. It doesn't make sense, but it does." She

166

hooked her arm though his and gave a tug. "Come on—let's keep going. Forward."

Beau nodded, not wanting to leave Bonnie behind, though for all he knew, she could be quite far from them already. They were quiet, their walk continuing and taking them over a very green moorside. It was once they had crossed the vastness of it and started climbing carefully over a barrage of smooth gray boulders that Beau began to notice that Audrey was suddenly and compulsively rubbing her hands down the front of her skirt. It was clear to him that her thoughts were exceptionally focused, almost painfully so.

"What are you thinking about?" he asked her then. She only shook her head, having cleared the rocks, and she continuing to walk and watch the path directly ahead of her. Still, the rubbing did not stop and she began to brush them together, wincing, and biting down against the slightest of whimpers as she did so. The act seemed to hurt her terribly and Beau's concern was growing at the sight of it.

"Audrey—" He stepped in front of her, catching her arms in his hands and when their eyes locked, he saw that she was not looking at him, but rather she was concentrating very hard on something else, and she would not stop walking, pushing him back as she went on. It was clear that there was far more happening than what he could see.

"Keep going-keep going-don't stop-don't stop—" she was muttering. "*Keep going-keep going-don't stop-don't stop—*" Beau got out of her way and let her go on, keeping at her side for every step. But she continued to rub her hands on her skirt, the motions suddenly leaving long, sticky, smeared red on it, the fabric soaking it up like a sponge. Still, Beau stayed out of her way, letting her continue.

They had covered nearly forty meters before she suddenly stopped and began to shake her hands out in front of her very hard, her brow drawn and extreme suffering across her face. Beau caught one of her hands in his and looked at her palm and then quickly glanced at the other: there were long, crimson streaks running across them from the web of her thumb to the opposite edge, and though they did not bleed through, it appeared that there were deep lacerations glowing beneath her skin, and the threads of red were running down her arms. That same blood had somehow escaped and was all over her dress.

"*What is that?*" he asked. She was back with him now and she shook her head, startled and a little frightened by the sight of it.

"I don't know!"

She shook her hands again and blew on them, as though it would make the fire in them stop by her cooling breath. And then, it suddenly left her.

Beau took her hands up again and the red marks were gone and there was not a trace that they had even been there but for the mess on her skirt.

"Was that from your sister?" he asked. Audrey nodded. "Is she alright?"

"I can still feel her," Audrey explained and had she not been all right, she was certain that she would either feel worse or she would probably feel a tremendous loss—and thankfully she felt neither.

"Do you want to stop for a moment?" Beau asked her. "Do you need to rest?"

"No—" Audrey shook her head, though she leaned on him for a moment, the entire exchange having been more intense than any she had shared with her sister in the past. "I wonder—what that was all about."

"I couldn't begin to guess."

After a few moments, Audrey was able to shake it off completely and they continued along the moors.

"Sometimes," she began, "it isn't so great to know what your twin is feeling."

Beau thought on her statement. He did not dislike feeling what Bonnie felt, though he did rather that she felt happy, peaceful and well, than full of anything to the contrary. He wondered for the hundredth time what it would be like to hear her thoughts: in the most non-intrusive way, of course.

"Does it help, being able to talk to your sister, without anyone being able to hear your conversation?"

"Quite often, yes."

"I suppose at times it must be very convenient."

"Absolutely."

They crested a hill and Audrey was the first to notice the building in the distance. She nodded to it and Beau took notice.

"That's our big top!" she exclaimed. But to Beau it was something quite different and something far more personal—it was his monastery. He did not argue, for the sake of seeing what it really was once they had reached it. As they arrived at the door, it was still her big top and still his monastery. He decided that it was whatever they were wanting it to be and as he knew that he wanted nothing more at that moment than to be home, Beau was certain that Audrey was putting the very same energies into the labyrinth. When they had gone inside, he made for the stairs to Bonnie's room, to see if perhaps she was there too.

"Beau—" He stopped at Audrey's calling to him and he turned at the sound of her voice. "Don't go far."

"You either."

And then he disappeared up the steps, taking them two and three at a time. He rushed down the hallway, knowing that if Bonnie was not there in her room, it was certain that she would be quick to follow. But when he reached her door, he was met with something he did not expect: her glass turret was not there *at all*. There was nothing there beyond the threshold but vast, open, midnight blackness with a few fading and twinkling stars in the great distance. His heart dropped and he believed it to be as gone as Bonnie's garret. He had not a second more to think about it, for Audrey's voice interrupted his thoughts and brought Beau directly back.

"Stop—stop. Stop! *Stop-now! Do-not-come-closer!"*

He hurried to her, flying down the stairs and into the main hall, coming to a most abrupt halt when he saw her in a face-off with a tiger nearly four times her size. It was in a deadlock stare with her, taking no notice of him at all, and the ground beneath their feet was rumbling with its growl.

"Audrey—" he whispered. "Where did that come from?" he asked.

"We're in the circus arena—" she whispered, not knowing that he was seeing a completely different environment. "What did you expect to find here?"

"So how do we get away from it?" he asked, still in a hushed voice.

"I don't think it can see you," she said. "At least, it isn't acting as though it can."

"Can't you talk to it? Don't you do things like that?"

"I tried. It can't seem to hear me—or it's ignoring me."

The tiger's growl came up in volume, and it took a step toward Audrey.

"The moment we move," she said, "It's going to come after us. Look around—do you see the stage doors on the left side of the arena?" Beau took a look, their views still conflicting.

"No but I see a walk-in fireplace."

"Well, whatever you think will be a good place to get into, where this tiger cannot follow us—"

"And then what?"

"You go to it. Run as fast as you can and do not look back. Do not even slow down because I'll be right behind you and we're going to be followed with not even a moment to blink."

"Alright. On the count of three, follow me. *One—*" He crept behind her. *"Two—"* And touched her shoulder reassuringly as he passed by her. *"Three—"*

Beau took off in a sprint as fast as he could, hoping that Audrey was right behind him and the temptation to look back to see if she was, was nearly unbearable. Beau made it into the fireplace, stepping into the side of it, hidden by the bricks. Within seconds, Audrey appeared and Beau grasped her with both hands, yanking her into the shadows with him. They were able to scrunch back farther, just escaping from the tiger's heavy, clawed swipe.

"I suppose the fact that this beast is at least twice the size of the fireplace we're in is a very good thing," Beau said. Audrey could only nod, trying to catch her breath, and cling to Beau as the tiger continued to swipe unsuccessfully, it's claws sparking with friction against the brick.

"So, are we stuck here until it goes away?" Beau asked.

"Not if the trap door is still here," Audrey answered, uncertain now as to where they really were, for she could smell the burnt wood and stone, the old ash settling on her skin.

"Where is it?"

"You're probably standing on it."

Beau let her stand in the far corner, safe from the tiger's reach, before he felt around on the floor of the fireplace. His fingers hooked onto the latch and Audrey sighed with relief at the sound of the metal hitting the wood.

"This must be it," Beau said, pulling it back.

It opened up to reveal a grassy, day-lit ground, several feet down. A tree trunk with boards nailed into it to form a ladder was within easy reach. Audrey peered down through the hole too, not expecting it to have gone anywhere but beneath the arena, and certainly she did not think she would see bright light.

"That is—interesting," she said.

"And I don't see any other tigers," Beau informed, lowering himself down to the first planked rung.

"Thank God for that," Audrey breathed, following him.

Chapter Eighteen
Seamus and Georgina

The field of irises gave way at long last to a new kind of field: this one was mechanical, metal and wooden, full of the interworkings of some sort of machinery. There were pipes and steam, glass panes and wooden beams and every bit of it was moving. Georgina stood at its edge with Seamus for a moment, he studying the entire thing carefully while being very still.

"Well, this is certainly a big mess," Georgina said.

"It isn't, actually."

"No?"

"No, look—"

He had her stand where he was standing, and he pointed to one particular area of it.

"I don't get it."

"Watch—" And he continued to point. "When the parts line up—"

She did watch for a moment, everything seeming to go at all different times and in different directions. She still believed it to be a great tangled mess of animated hardware. But then Georgina too saw what Seamus had discovered: at a very precise moment, all of it would synchronize and a very direct hall was made through it. And at the very end of that hall, was a door with an awaiting spot for a lock and a key.

"Ah. *Now* I see it!" she said and Seamus smiled so widely, she thought he might burst into an explosion of light. "Now, how do we get to it?"

"We will have to go slowly," he explained, taking her hand so they could start toward their goal. "I don't know how much you know about machinery—"

"Not much," she admitted.

"Well, that's alright. You have to think of this structure we're going into as a something like a heart: everything is pumping and working together to keep it going. If one little thing gets out of sync or hiccups, it could get complicated."

"Hm. Sounds complicated already," she said, noticing that there was nothing below any of their walkways but endless blue sky.

"Well, it shouldn't be—we just have to pay attention. *Very close* attention. And don't lose your balance."

Georgina followed Seamus exactly, taking every step he took, ducking every time he ducked and never letting go of his hand, to be sure that they did not get separated: they were much too far along in the maze and with their way out so close—she did not even want to think of the consequences did something happen to disrupt the rhythm of things, or if one or both of them took a false step and lost their footing. It seemed to all go off well enough, but the deeper into it that they became, the quicker the moving parts seemed to go.

"It's as though it's beating faster," Georgina said. "I know *my* heart is going faster."

"Mine too."

And still, as they progressed, so did the adrenaline of the mechanisms. Georgina and Seamus picked up their pace, their muscles clenched as they tried to hurry but keep the most careful of traction.

They both felt that their own hearts might explode, did they not come to the door soon, but they did before long, find themselves just a leap away from it. The trick was not in traversing it, but in doing so with no running room for the jump.

"How are we going to do this?" she asked Seamus, wishing that the deafening, plunging and pounding of pistons and such behind and over them would stop for just a moment so they could hear themselves think.

"We're just going to have to jump—"

"Right. Just jump. Okay. You want to go first?" she offered.

"Sure."

But when Seamus jumped, he did not clear it. Georgina gasped, instinctively reaching out for him, though she could not even get a fraction of the distance to him. He hung onto a steaming, spitting pipe, pain drawn across his face as he felt it and he had to alternate which hand he held it with.

"*Jump, Georgina!*" he yelled. She hesitated, unsure as to what she should do. "You'll make it—" he insisted. "*Hurry, please—!*"

She saw one of his palms as he let go, the threads of the pipe having marked his skin. He was not going to hold on much longer: and she jumped.

Georgina landed hard on the metal grate, ignoring that the sharpness of it scraped her knees like razors and she crawled to Seamus, grasping his free hand.

"Swing up—" she instructed, wishing he would get another part of him—*any* part of him close enough to her that she could grab hold.

"Take my key—" he was saying. And though she easily could have taken it, Georgina could not help but feel a little insulted that he was giving up so easily.

"Get up here!" she hollered at him. "I am *not* answering to your brother, so *get up here!*"

Seamus's hand let go of the pipe then and Georgina had to dig her heels into the grate so she would not slide off of it with him.

"*Dammit, Seamus!*" She grit her teeth against his pulling, wishing all of his movement would give him enough momentum to swing himself up beside her. She felt that her arms were going to disjoint and her wrists were going to snap, the weight of him becoming more and more real with his stirring about. The giant machine began to fall apart then, parts of all kinds coming undone and thudding down with gravity's pull. It seemed to be giving up and looked to take them with it. Georgina closed her eyes, clenching her teeth more tightly together, wishing it to be over in whatever manner it was meant to. And then it was:

Seamus wrenched his wrist free, letting go of her and Georgina cried out, her eyes opening at the hard thump and crash on the grate beside her:

He had waited for just the perfect and plummeting something to fall past him, stepping up onto it with lightening speed as it fell to get just a bit higher up, and then swung himself just hard enough that he was able to throw himself up onto the platform.

Georgina grabbed him and held onto him, Seamus smiling as he breathed hard, but closing his eyes to catch his breath. When they were both sure that they were not going to go down with the mechanical beast, they stood on shaky legs and went the last few feet to the door.

"You know—for all of the hard work this has been: it certainly has been fun," Seamus admitted, taking his key off from around his neck. Somehow, though she had been along for every moment of their struggle, and though she deeply wanted to, Georgina could not disagree at all. They both looked at the door and their key and lock.

"Are you ready to leave?" he asked her.

"You know, I don't think I am," she said half-truthfully.

"There is always the chance we could come back," he suggested.

"Well, if there is always the chance of *that*," Georgina said. "Then I suppose I've had quite enough for now."

Upon their agreement, they put Georgina's lock into the door and the key into the lock, both of them smiling when Seamus turned it.

Chapter Nineteen
Audrey and Beau

Audrey was the first to see the coins when they reached the ground, and they were presumably gold and shining, though they were in a sluggish stream of green stickiness. She dropped to her knees the moment she reached it, watching the slow flow of it, the coins turning over and catching in the light.

"What do you suppose they're in?" she asked Beau, her excitement at their discovery very apparent.

"Honey."

"What?" she asked absently, having a hard time looking away from them.

"Honey. It's green honey."

"How do you know this? Not that it matters, really—it's all so lovely!"

"I do know my bees. Oh—" And something else caught his eye.

"If you say so—"

Beau turned her head to look at what he was seeing: a door like the one they'd entered the maze through, a hollow awaiting their lock and key.

"Oh," she breathed, realizing what it was.

Beau started toward the door, stirring up an awaiting sentry of black and green bees. He stilled as they swarmed around him. He looked at the door, seeing that he was very close to it. But he needed Audrey there too.

"Audrey—" he said, looking back at her. She was still enraptured by the coins and not appearing interested in anything else.

"Yes—" but her voice was removed, her eyes snagged narcissistically.

"The door—it's the way out of the maze—"

"Oh?" No movement.

Beau began to fear that they might never get out—and being so close! He wanted to go back to Audrey and grab her—drag her if had to, to the door, but the bees were building a thick wall between Audrey and himself. His mind raced and his heart was longing for Bonnie again.

"Audrey—we've got to leave. We don't have much time—"

"So much—there is *so much* gold here—"

"It's not real," he found himself saying, though whether it was true or not, he didn't know.

"Not real?" she asked, still entranced, though not as amorously.

"No, not real. But the door *is* real. And your sister, Aubrey is real. She's waiting for you on the other side of the door."

"Aubrey—"

"I know you want to see her. And I need to see Bonnie! *Please*, Audrey. I want to be home with Bonnie."

"Bonnie—your sister."

"*Yes*." And he could finally hear her beginning to rise. "My sister."

"And Aubrey."

"*Yes*."

She was just on the other side of the bees.

"We can go to them now," Beau said.

But when she tried to step around the wall, they followed, blocking her still.

"I can't get through—" she whispered.

"Yes you can. You have to just come straight through."

"But I'm allergic to bees, Beau!"

"So am I," Beau said, hoping it was not true, for though he had spent many years around them, he had never once been stung: he really did not know. "Come on, Audrey. They won't hurt you."

And he very carefully and very slowly stuck his hand through the bees. They parted, more curious than aggressive and when she took his hand and he pulled her through them, they did not sting; their humming wings and buzzing blowing cool on her. When she was safely with Beau, he smiled at her.

"They're happy you didn't take their gold," he stated. Audrey looked a bit distraught. "Our sisters—" he said, refocusing her, for at the mention of the gold she had been lost again to their goal. She sighed, a little relived.

"Our sisters."

They went to the door together—Beau's lock, Audrey's key—and their hearts skipped at the sound of the clicking in the lock.

Chapter Twenty
Bonnie and Ianto

Bonnie was going toward the cottage even before Ianto, the rising breeze lifting her hair and blowing it about her face. She looked back at him, seeing that he followed along closely, his eyes catching with hers and his smile growing. But with this, the wind began to pick up, and it made her hair whip across her face, stinging and blinding her eyes. She laughed to herself, it reminding her of the day she had been found by Beau—the wind having been the same way. She thought it to be a great omen that she was very close to her brother just then and she persisted, her hands catching the tresses as much as she could and holding them down. Only a few more steps and Bonnie found that the wind was turning into very strong gales, threatening to push her back away from the cottage before she could get too close. She went on, squinting against the dust that was stirred and holding a hand out before her, leaves and even small twigs coming down at them. She stopped smiling then, both seeing the hole in the door for Ianto's lock and wondering if they were about to set up against another challenge before they could get to it. It was with this very thought that she wondered if she had imagined Ianto calling her name from behind her, or if he really had, when a violent gust swept around her like an invisible hand and took her off of her feet and into the air. The world around her seemed to shove ahead of Bonnie—taking Ianto with it— or perhaps it was forcing her backward. Bonnie was questioning to herself just how far she was going to be carried when she was dropped hard to the ground. She held her hand to the back of her head where it had hit hard onto rock, looking for Ianto and seeing that he had stopped walking but was now far ahead of her, looking back her way. She stood slowly, the wind never stopping and it was reluctant in letting her catch up with Ianto. Still, she tried, pushing and pushing, stumbling and regaining her footing, swearing stubbornly to herself that she would crawl to the door if she had to. With this thought, the current gave more resistance, throwing freezing rain at her. She pulled her hood up and grasped it tightly, keeping her eyes closed and only opening them every few steps to see that she was still going in the right direction. She could see that Ianto was trying to backtrack to her, but as the wind did not want her getting to him, it did not want him getting to Bonnie either, and he was stuck where he was. It made her want to bridge the gap between them all the more and she pressed on with determined insistence.

The ice-rain turned to heavy snow, white and unyielding, biting and so cold that Bonnie felt it wanted her to turn into a living statue. She would not give in, thinking only of getting to Ianto, for at the very least she knew he could provide warmth. It was futile, but she could not help trying to wipe the flakes from her face, for they were only replaced by more and more, raw and leaving scrapes across her cheeks. She wanted to get to Ianto. She wanted to get to Beau and she wanted to get home. Nothing sounded lovelier to her just then than her diamond turret and the thick, soft covers on her bed, or the glow of a candle burning from across the room. The entire vision was so terribly sweet and inviting—Bonnie wanted to sink into the warmth of it and sleep and sleep and sleep in the soft, heaven of it. She felt the torrents of wind lessen and she was lowered to the ground, whether on her own accord or from the storm letting her down, she couldn't tell. But really it did not matter—she would just rest there for a moment, Bonnie thought. Close her eyes and rest, because now the blanket of snow was becoming heavy on top of her, but it was faithfully blocking out the wind and so she would give it what it wanted: her.

Ianto had kept his eyes on Bonnie for as long as he could, while he was held captive at the wall of wind. He had cringed when she had fallen from the air and he nearly held his breath as he saw her persist in his direction. The rain had started, falling only toward her it had seemed, for he had remained unassaulted by it. Still, she had continued. The snow had followed, blocking her from his view, but he hoped she would endure it enough to get closer.

He could no longer see her and the snow was increasing in depth around his legs. It was heavy, wet snow, and even when he felt the wind lift just slightly, for the blizzard was busily dumping down its contents, he was able to wade through it very slowly. He knew it would take a long while to go to where he thought he had seen Bonnie last, but did he take his time, he might have a better chance of not drawing attention to himself. It was odd—thinking the wind as an entity and not so much as an element, but fire often acted in such a way, why not the wind? It was with this last thought that he felt his legs suddenly stopped and blocked by something on the ground, and it was just warm enough to give him hope.

Bonnie was not certain where her thoughts were taking her, but it was something like a dreamy wave and she was going to let it take her along with it. But then it was interrupted and she felt the darkness give way to light, the open air refreshing but still so cold. She was lifted into strong and warm arms, the beating of a heart against her cheek as she was cradled against it, becoming more and more real to her. Her numb fingers began to feel cloth beneath them and they slipped between overlapping folds to touch skin that was warmer still.

Ianto gasped at the cold touch of Bonnie's fingers on his chest, but he was relieved that she was conscious and he did not mind it one bit.

"If you're trying to get into my pocket, love, it's on the outside of my shirt," he played. Bonnie was waking slowly, but she had heard him.

"I'm trying to get into your heart," she whispered. Ianto thought he would nearly drop her at her words for the sweet shock of them, but they made him hold her even more tightly to him.

"You're already in there, Bonnie," he whispered back.

She smiled, filling with such a bliss she wondered if she was going to cry. But she did not and instead asked him if she should get on her own feet and walk the rest of the way.

"I am not letting you down until we are at the door," he said to her. "We are going to get there together."

Truthfully, he did not mind carrying her and Bonnie was thankful for not having to walk—she was not so sure she could feel her legs enough yet to even try.

"Is it close?" she asked softly.

"Quite."

She snuggled closer to him for the rest of the distance and Ianto held her for a moment more even after he stepped up to the door, closing his eyes and breathing her in. He sighed and kissed the top of her head.

"Are you ready, love?" She nodded and Ianto set Bonnie down, her feet and legs much stronger than she had expected them to be.

He put his lock in the door and Bonnie put her key into it, thinking of how different she felt at that door than she had the last time she and Ianto were faced with the same sort of instance. She smiled when he put his hand over hers as she held the key and they turned it together.

Chapter Twenty-One
Gabriel and Aubrey

W hen Gabriel and Aubrey reached the first door, or rather where the thought the door ought to have been— there was no door at all.

"See?" she said. "I told you: *mirage.*"

"Not so fast, little madam," Gabriel said, walking back and forth where the flashing was supposed to have been.

"I'm getting tired, Gabe. I was kind of hoping for this bit to go on a little faster than the rest has so far."

"I should think that this would go fast," he remarked. "Do you see anything between here and the next flashy thing?"

"Just lots and lots of sand and rock."

"So we should have no trouble getting to each one."

"No—" Aubrey said hesitantly.

"Oh, I don't like the sound of that," Gabriel said in reference to her tone. But quickly following it was a rumble in the ground beneath their moving feet. "I especially don't like the sound of *that.*"

Aubrey stopped, pulling Gabriel to stop along with her. The rumbling grew and rippled across the surface they stood on, the reverberation traveling up the giant rock pillars and making them tremble in their poses.

"Earthquake?" Aubrey wondered out loud.

"Are we even still on earth? You know it looks more like mars—"

"Hush!" Aubrey interrupted. "*Please* do not wish that on us."

Before Gabriel could say anything to that, one of the rock stacks began to topple over, the incredibly sized boulders causing everything to shake when they hit the desert floor. It started an immense domino effect, the mounds taking their turn in collapsing. It was not enough that their new positioning made it impossible for Gabriel and Aubrey to see any more of their suspected doors, but the crumpling was growing closer and closer to where they stood.

"Gabe! What should we do?" Aubrey asked frantically.

"We should probably run—"

"But where to? They're everywhere and they're all coming down!"

"Probably toward the ones that are already down."

"That's crazy—"

"Well, there has to be an interception at some point. And I don't know about you, but I can't outrun them. So—we may as well catch up and pass them."

He grabbed her hand and began pulling her along with him, dodging the falling rocks with some kind of grace that Aubrey never would have suspected Gabriel to have in him. They had to go around and over the already fallen rocks, some of them having fallen into a straight line and Gabriel had to boost Aubrey up on top of them. When the quaking had ended near them and the rumbling had passed into the far off distance, they paused on top of a boulder to search out the flashings in the settling dust.

"Still there—" Gabriel indicated, pointing to them. He jumped down and helped Aubrey to descend. "Well at least we know that the last one we check will be the right one."

"So then let's check the last one next," she said, trying to keep her humor.

Gabriel grinned and shook his finger at her.

"Process of elimination can't be done backwards."

"We just barely escaped being crushed by the biggest pebbles I've ever seen—*we've* ever seen. How can you be so sure?"

"Well—" He stopped, taking her hand again as they walked. "I suppose I can't be sure."

"You see there?"

"All right, let's make a deal: I'll agree that it may be possible for the process of elimination to work in reverse, *if* you agree that one of these flashing whatevers is our way back out."

"Deal."

And just as Gabriel had said it would be, the last flashing they found was in fact a door. It was copper and shone so brightly in the light that had it been golden instead, they would have thought that they were about to be walking right into the sun.

"It's the most beautiful door I've ever seen," Aubrey breathed.

"I could not agree more," Gabriel responded, letting her go first to put her lock into it. His key came next and she turned it.

Chapter Twenty-Two
Duality

December 1st, 12:02 Ante Meridiem

Night was the only light on the circular courtyard. It was at a precise and exact moment that the four doors circling it unlocked and opened, and each one revealed a slowly emerging couple.

Audrey and Aubrey saw one another immediately, both knowing that their sibling would be there. They ran to one another, embracing and nearly knocking one another over before they took notice of the muddied, shredded and bloodied state their dresses were in. They began to converse all in a silent storm of words, unheard by anyone else there.

Gabriel and Georgina gave one another a smirk, an exaggerated rolling of the eyes and at last some semblance of a smile, but they kept their distance, choosing to laugh at the filthy and otherwise destroyed condition of one another's clothing instead of exchanging sentiments.

Bonnie and Beau's eyes met at a distance, just as they had so many years before that moment and a flooding of emotion came over them both. They were hesitant to approach one another, already having been tricked once by the maze and it was agonizing to be reliving that moment. Ianto's heart bled for Bonnie and her brother for it, remembering too well how it had been for her. He caressed her face and kissed her before he smiled and took her hand, leading her to Beau. When they were close enough, he placed their hands together and stepped back when Beau lifted Bonnie up in his arms, crushing her affectionately.

Seamus met up with his brother in the middle of the courtyard then. They shook hands and then hugged one another as well, laughing and sharing in their victory: for though they had not built the frame of the labyrinth, it was as Bonnie had said—it was theirs still.

And now it belonged to all of them.

Additional Thank You's

A gi-normous thank you to SarHa Minch, Meredith
Frye, Linda Hutsell, Jen Parrish and Ed Walters:
For reading this—pre-publication—upon my acquiesced
request.

A gracious thank you to Jodi Vargo: for your undying
cheer, and to Chris Schanz, Merle "Little Peasy" Pace
and Carrie Sandoval: for your beautiful inspiration and
for cosseting my muse.

An honorable thank you to Butch Cavity, Tori Amos,
Muse, Placebo, Keane, The Cure, Stereophonics,
Evanescence, The Cardigans, Coldplay, Enigma and
various other musical artists and groups who
unknowingly helped to carry the most perfect of vibes
throughout this entire story as I wrote it.

A hospitable thank you to the Carpe Diem guest house
of Provincetown, Massachussetts and
Jaho's coffee house of Salem, Massachussetts:
Where I spent quite a bit of time scribbling out the tale
within.

And a very special thank you to NaNoWriMo.org for
providing the program that helped to get this going,
and to Linda Blackwood:
Without your plea to me of *"LET THE TWINS
LIVE*!!"—the key that opened the locked door to all of
this—this story might never have been written.

CPSIA information can be obtained at www.ICGtesting.com
Printed in the USA
LVOW05s2233100214

373175LV00001B/219/P

9 780578 018430